### IAN WOODHEAD
# PTERANODON MALL

SEVERED PRESS
HOBART TASMANIA

# PTERANODON MALL

Copyright © 2016 Ian Woodhead
Copyright © 2016 Severed Press

*WWW.SEVEREDPRESS.COM*

All rights reserved. No part of this book may be reproduced or transmitted in any form or by any electronic or mechanical means, including photocopying, recording or by any information and retrieval system, without the written permission of the publisher and author, except where permitted by law.

This novel is a work of fiction. Names, characters, places and incidents are the product of the author's imagination, or are used fictitiously. Any resemblance to actual events, locales or persons, living or dead, is purely coincidental.

*ISBN: 978-1-925493-57-3*

All rights reserved.

# CHAPTER ONE

Its bright green eyes locked upon the animal's large bulk. Although the potential prey out-massed the hunter by three, this apparent disadvantage had not dissuaded this animal from seeking a smaller, less dangerous prey, perhaps an animal that was not equipped with such a formidable-looking spiked tail.

Dailess-Zaid leaned closer to the viewcrystal, feeling most proud and honoured to be watching one of his ancient ancestors in its natural environment, stalking its food. He took his own large green eyes away from the view and compared his digits to those of the hunter, attempting to visualise to evolutionary transition between him and that creature. Millions of years separated the two species, and although Dailess-Zaid had lost his tail and his head no longer protruded, he still saw the similarity between him and this hunter.

He looked up at his three trophy heads displayed on the wall above his control system. These three were of his species, and as a direct comparison, the evolutionary transition now became evident. Dailess-Zaid did find it ironic that here he was, millions of years in his past, comparing the heads of a bunch of terrorists to a creature that they themselves wanted to revert to.

The Sons of Maulis-Bow pronounced the changes which time and circumstance had wrought upon their species an utter travesty. They believed that only in their true form would the Great Deity accept their Ka into the hunting ground. The terrorists obviously had something missing from their stupid little minds, and as far as he was concerned, they should all be tracked down and exterminated for believing in such puerile nonsense. They wanted to get back to their true form via the use of genetic manipulation. He made the sign of the circle and asked the Great Deity for forgiveness for even thinking of the black science.

He looked down, watching the hunter shift its weight onto the other leg. Dailess-Zaid attempted to forget about some terrorist organisation which would not even arise for another sixty-five million years and settled down, eager to watch this confrontation to the end. He ran his black tongue across his upper teeth, feeling the blood in his veins warm in anticipation.

The prey animal shivered. It lifted its head and swung it from side to side. A deep roar issued from its mouth. It too shifted its weight but in panic. Had it sensed the hunter? Dailess-Zaid hoped not. He wanted to see the kill. Dailess-Zaid needed to see it. In all honesty, he would have sold two of his pairing mates into slavery to actually be outside the protective shell of the quantum displacer.

Hot saliva dribbled down the sides of his mouth as he imagined himself being in the place of that hunter, about to leap upon the prey animal's back and sink his sharp teeth into its thick hide.

The Sons of Maulis-Bow would have taken this urging to be the ultimate proof that their species should not have evolved beyond that magnificent creature out there, and that to have gained sentience was the greatest catastrophe ever inflicted upon their species. Their obsession with the past did not stop them from attempting to acquire advanced military equipment to help them further their cause, though. If they really did believe all technical advancements to be heresy and an affront to the Great Deity, then why did they not attack their targets using only their claws and teeth? He would have enjoyed seeing such a spectacle. Perhaps if such an event had occurred, he might even join in with their enthusiasm and order his clan guard to leave the pulse blasters in their sheaths and killed them using only their claws and teeth.

The prey animal shook its massive body before turning to the side. The tail swung from side to side, those four spikes effectively protecting its rear. The twin plates running all the way down its back now glowed a bright red. Dailess-Zaid heard another growl. It took him a moment to realise the noise came from him. He then almost fell off his perch in surprise when three more hunters streaked out from the thick undergrowth and leaped upon the prey animal's back. Two of them biting into those plates, while one more managing to find a hold on its tender side.

The creature roared out in pain and shook its huge body in an attempt to dislodge the three hunters. His own body ached to be out there, joining his ancient brethren, helping them to take this animal down. His mind calmly informed him that if he was in amongst those beasts, the hunters would not hesitate to turn on him. The feeling of kinship which he shared with these hunters would not be reciprocated. They would kill him before returning to tear into the larger prey animal.

He sighed in pleasure when the original hunter darted out from its hiding place and took the prey animal completely by surprise. It fastened its jaws around the side of the creature's head and bit down. All motion in the prey animal ceased and it fell to the ground, almost flattening two of the hunters.

Dailess-Zaid saw two amber lights flashing to the side of the viewcrystal. He flicked his tongue in annoyance before his claws danced across the console. The image of the ship's secondary clan master Quediss-Tel replaced the pleasing views of the hunters settling down to feast. He flicked his tongue over his snout to display annoyance at this fool's wanton disregard for obeying a superior's order.

"It surprises me, Quediss-Tel, to find your ugly head contaminating my view. It is almost as if you wish me to strip you of your rank."

The senior officer bowed his head to the required level to show his servitude and gratification for the honour of being able to listen to Dailess-Zed's bluntness. It struck him as a little odd to find the senior officer having the courage to disturb the ship commander on his rest period. Whatever it was, the call must be important. Quediss-Tel might not be the most intelligent of his officers, but the male certainly was not a fool.

"You have my permission to speak," he said, trying not to lose his temper. Thanks to this call, he had lost the only chance he would ever get to watch a pack of his ancestors eat in their natural environment. Oh, Dailess-Zaid was fully aware that he would still be able to see them hunter, kill and eat again. After all, their cryo-tanks were overflowing with many species of ancient creatures, all packed and ready for the scientists when they get back to their own time. "Well, do you have a report for me, or are you going to remain mute?"

The senior officer finally lifted his head. The look of terror firmly etched upon his snout. Dailess-Zaid lost all his annoyance at being disturbed. He stood and leaned closer to the viewcrystal. "I said *report*!"

"We found an intruder hiding in the engine room, sir. He says he belongs to the Sons of Maulis-Bow." The officer paused. "Sir, he says he has planted an explosive device which will detonate when we spin up to the last cycle."

"What?" he thundered. "But that is imminent. Why was I not informed earlier?"

"It took us quite a while to torture this information out of the prisoner, sir. You ordered us not to disturb you."

Both he and the senior officer looked directly above them as the hull ceiling changed colour, indicating the last cycle had begun. Dailess-Zaid was thrown back into his perch as the temporal blast surged through his ship. He gripped the side of the perch, already aware that something had gone very wrong.

## CHAPTER TWO

Jefferson Wade reached for the milkshake, ripped off the plastic cap, and poured a quarter of the freezing sludge down his throat. He blinked away his tears and took a deep breath before placing the cup next to his half-eaten burger. None of his companions had even noticed he almost choked. What kind of friends did he have here?

Both Sandy Elmer and Alan Drake were too busy listening to Jefferson's workmate bang on about the shoplifter he caught a couple of days ago. He idly flicked a piece of lettuce across the black counter, wondering if he ought to ask David to hush up, if only for a moment. At least until he had remembered to get his story right.

Sandy's blue eyes flickered towards the multiple fans above their tables in the mall's eatery, and a hint of a smile appeared on Alan's face when Davis got to the part where he wrestled this huge guy to the ground and sat on him until security arrived.

Apart from their table, Jefferson spotted some old lady who worked at Martin's Department Store at the other end of the mall's eatery. She was currently drinking her tea, while a young woman bent over a pushchair fed mushed-up stuff from a pink plastic container into the mouth of a toddler. She wasn't having much success. Jefferson had to look away, feeling his face redden by the sight of her large breasts pressed against her low-cut blue top. Did she have no shame? Perhaps it was a good job his mate was too busy embellishing his lie to notice her. David would have had no problems in staring.

He did wonder who she was though, considering the mall had yet to open. Unless her boyfriend or husband worked here. Not that it was any of his concern. Still, it posed a bit of a mystery, and it was certainly better than listening to this crappy story again.

Sandy had stood. She collected Alan's burger wrapper and her sushi container, and popped it on her tray. David had now reached the point where he was making his report to the police. Jefferson sighed. From the way he told it, anyone would think that this little glasses-wearing guy, with his fluffy brown hair and arms like the drumsticks on David's full paper plate, was actually a superhero in disguise.

"It's a bloody good disguise," he muttered behind his milkshake.

"Okay, guys. I'd better depart."

Sandy gave Dave the biggest condescending smile that Jefferson had ever seen before taking her tray over to the bin.

Alan grabbed his coat. He straightened his multi-coloured tie before extracting himself from between the table and the bench.

"Wait up, I'll walk with you."

Jefferson sighed again while trying not to allow his raging libido to turn his head back to the woman feeding her kid. Instead, he watched his two mates walk over to their relevant shops. Sandy worked in the nail bar, situated at the front of Tailor's Beauty Parlour. From his till point in the PoundSave discount shop, Jefferson could watch the girl work her magic on some of the trogs who frequented her booth.

Alan worked in the next shop, David's favourite haunt in the whole mall. Well, apart from the eatery, that is. Alan had the dubious honour of being the assistant manager in the mall's only toy shop.

Sandy was getting married in less than a month, and Alan's boyfriend was a gym instructor. Watching those two walk together, anyone would think they were a couple, short of holding hands, that is. Jefferson's gaze turned from the pretend couple, bypassed David filling his mouth with fried chicken, and watched the woman walk past his table. Her slim hands wrapped around the pushchair handles.

Here he was, twenty-three years old, working in the crappiest job in the universe, single, and poor. Here he was, sitting next to a lad who still lived with his mum, couldn't stop lying, and collected toy cars. Jefferson stuck his forefinger into the last bits of pale goop at the bottom of the plastic cup and pushed a lump of ice cream around the base. He wanted something exciting to happen in his boring life.

The woman stopped a few feet from his table and bent over again. Oh Christ, was she doing this on purpose?

Jefferson pinched a couple of fries from David's plate. "Seven foot, dude? Seriously?"

David didn't answer back, he just shovelled the last fries into his mouth, and grinned.

Jefferson seriously wondered if it was possible to die from sighing too much. "Come on, gobshite. We'd better make tracks ourselves. You know how pissy Mr. Hussain gets if we're not there on time."

"Will you stop fretting, man? We have another seven minutes left. It only takes one of them to traverse the distance from this establishment to the sweatshop. Plenty of time to demolish the food still remaining on my plate."

"I think I hate my life."

His mate grinned again. Thankfully, Jefferson noted that this time David had at least swallowed his mouth contents first.

"You worry too much." David picked up the last two chicken nuggets, grabbed his coat, and joined Jefferson beside the fresh doughnut stall. "Did you see the way Sandy smiled at me, Jeffdude? Trust me, she wants my body."

"I wish you wouldn't call me that." Jefferson picked up the pace when he noticed their boss's familiar green baseball cap by the front entrance. He grabbed David's arm and pulled him over to their shop and booted him inside, while Mr. Hussain was busy chatting to the security guard. It didn't shock him to see it was Mo this morning, the lad who had pulled the shoplifter off David yesterday afternoon.

"Stop it with the manhandling, Jeffdude. I can make my own way, thank you very much."

He followed David through the shop and into the back area, nodding at Gloria, their supervisor. She smiled back then continued to drop the change into the tills.

"Well, what do you think?"

Jefferson swiped his staff-card down the clock machine. "About you chatting crap about your imagined escapades?"

"What? No, I mean about me and Sandy. You reckon I have a chance?"

"Jesus. What part of *she is getting married* do you not get? You'd have a better chance asking me out."

David chuckled. "You have a crazy sense of humour, Jeffdude." He clocked in too before waltzing through the doors and back into the shop. Jefferson listened to his mate compliment Gloria on her lovely hair, just like he did every morning. As tradition demanded, the woman, who was old enough to be David's mum, giggled and called him lover boy. It took a lot of effort to stop him from sighing again.

Jefferson clipped on his name tag, pushed open the staffroom door, and walked onto the shop-floor, ready to face whatever today would throw at him. Only he wasn't ready. Jefferson wasn't ready at all. Unlike that empty-headed buffoon, currently playing tiddlywinks with a couple of pennies, Jefferson didn't intend to spend the rest of his life lusting after Sandy or spending stupid amounts of money on toy cars.

He squeezed past Gloria, noting that she wore that *God awful* perfume again. Jefferson held his breath while he took up position by his till. He decided there and then that tradition could go *fuck itself* this lunchtime. Instead of joining the others at their designated table in the eatery, Jefferson would grab a sandwich in the cafe in Martin's Department Store. He had to admit, that idea did have legs. He hadn't been in there for weeks. It would be a pleasant change to be alone with his thoughts for once, without having to listen to David's stories, or Alan's current beef with his fella, or Sandy bitching about the trogs who came to have their nails done. Just him, a beef sandwich, and a window to gaze out.

Then again, it might be a better idea to leave the mall altogether and grab a pasty from Greggs instead. The fresh air would do him the world of good, and after spending next four hours next to Gloria, Jefferson would need a ton of the stuff to sandblast the stink of her perfume from his lungs.

Someone ought to tell the woman that she smelled like a cross between a vanilla wax-melt and brake fluid. Jefferson would give that job to David. He'd do it as well, the empty-headed buffoon.

The thought of this woman punching out David's lights did bring a smile to his face. He'd like to see how he'd explain that to the gang at tomorrow's meeting at their table.

## CHAPTER THREE

The brats had finally skulked off to their respective shops; it took them long enough. Another few minutes, and Desmond Lampton would have been forced to put his foot down and use his authority.

Not that Desmond had any real power. He would have just stood beside their table, tapping on his sweeping brush, until they took the bloody hint and buggered off. The good-for-nothing, bone-idle brats. They wouldn't know real work if it smacked them all in the chops.

He reached their table, wondering if he should have done that anyway. That chick who worked in the nail-bar was hot. He'd give his left eye to spend some quality time in the sack with that prize piece of arse. Desmond might have to make a few more discreet inquiries about that one, to see if he could find out where she lived.

The gobby kid, who worked with that shifty-looking bastard in the discount store, had left a chicken drumstick. Desmond casually dropped that into his special bag before cleaning away the rest of the crap that the messy little bastards had left.

It shouldn't be allowed. That's all he had to say on the matter. They sloped in here with their noise, unsightly hair, and general shitty behaviour, and left their crap all over his spotless table. All without giving a toss about it. It would be poor Desmond here who'd get in trouble if the shift manager paid the eatery a surprise inspection.

Desmond gave the table a swift wipe before removing himself from the eatery. He didn't like it here. There were too many kids around, and they were the ones who served the food. It was time to make a quick exit before even more of the pint-sized fuckers streamed through that door. Desmond absolutely detested Saturday morning in the Hopeview Shopping Mall.

He made his way along the main concourse, pushing his cleaning trolley ahead of him. The rear wheel on his left squeaked. This told him that his mate, Henry Wild, had switched trolleys again, the shithead. Desmond grinned. He didn't blame the old bastard. After all, he'd switched them in the first place last week.

There were still a few more minutes before opening time, so it gave him just enough time to slow down and stop right outside the beauty shop's front window, hoping to catch a glimpse of the hot chick again.

He couldn't see her. Bloody hell, what a disappointment. Desmond pressed his face against the glass, wondering where she was. He almost jumped out of his skin at the sound of someone banging on the window. It didn't come from this shop, though. He stood back to discover that blond twerp from the toy shop scowling at him. The twerp stood there, amongst a display of Legos, giving Desmond daggers.

He grabbed the handles of his trolley, stared at the black and white tiles, and pushed his trolley past both shops while grinding his teeth. If it wasn't for the fact that without this crappy job, where he'd probably end up sleeping rough again, he would have marched right in there and punch that clown right in the chops.

"None of these kids have any respect for me," he muttered.

Henry always told him to lighten up whenever Desmond got like this, reminding him that they were exactly the same at their age. He'd flash those stumpy teeth, blast out that rotting-meat breath, and call him a miserable old bastard.

He reached the new car display and turned left, heading towards the restroom area. Maybe Henry did have a point. He did admit that recently the tolerance for these kids had reached an all-time low. Thing is, he just couldn't help himself. Just being close to anyone under the age of twenty-five made him want to either hit them or, if they were pretty, take them to bed. The chances of doing either were slim to none, not if wanted to keep this shit job or wanted to go to prison.

Desmond stopped by the restroom corridor. He waited for some older man wearing a Martin's Department Store uniform to pass him before opening his special bag. Along with the chicken, he had also collected a slice of meat feast pizza, two burger meat patties, and a lump of spicy beef. He left out the fries.

He knew for a fact that his new pet wouldn't eat those. Desmond had second thoughts about the pizza too. From what he'd found out, little Joey wasn't keen on anything but meat.

None of this stuff was for him, despite what Henry thought. He grinned to himself, remembering the old man's face when he'd noticed Desmond's special bag last night. Just like that nosey old bastard, Henry had swiped the bag off the trolley and opened it up, chuckling at the sight of the two pieces of fried chicken that Desmond had swiped from a table just ten minutes earlier.

Last night, though, was a bit of a strange time for him. For last night was when he found the little bird; at least, that's what it looked like.

The bloke from the department store hadn't even noticed this cleaner. Desmond could have stood here in his birthday suit and that clown wouldn't have paid the slightest bit of attention, not that this came as a surprise to him. Still, it paid dividends to be careful.

On his shift, last night, he had come across what had to be the weirdest thing he had ever found on his travels. Desmond was quite used to finding dropped money, watches, phones, even underwear. He considered that to be a perk of the job. The guy behind the bar in the Lamb and Flag paid well for some of the gear he brought in. Not the underwear, though. That went in the bin, unless it was from some female teen; that ended up under his bed.

Of all the gear he had found, nothing compared to the pretty bird that had poked its head out from under one of the cubicles in the gents. After putting his racing heart back where it lived, Desmond crouched gently swinging the door inwards so he could see the rest of it. He had frowned. He'd frowned a lot. Although it was covered in red and blue feathers and had bird feet, hell, it even sounded like a sparrow. It clearly wasn't a bird, not with teeth like that.

For the first time in weeks, Desmond laughed out loud at the sight of this weird little animal cocking its head to one side while chirping like a sparrow. Looking back, that had been a very dumb idea as he must have shocked the life out of it.

The bird's feathery arms pushed forwards, showing Desmond those hooked claws before it ran straight for his face. His old army training kicked in just in time, and he fell to the side, hitting his head on the tiles. A slight bump to his head was better than losing his nose to those teeth or it turning his cheeks into bloodied ribbons.

Desmond snapped his arm towards the bird and wrapped his fingers around the squawking creature's neck. He gave it a gentle squeeze, grinning when it suddenly stopped making all that headache-inducing noise. Despite his brush with a trip to A&E, Desmond was still chuckling away. His find was dangerous, mean-tempered and unpredictable, just like him.

He'd got himself a new pet, something weird and nasty, a meat-eater, that's for sure. Desmond had no idea how it had gotten into the toilets or where it had appeared from. At first, he assumed the bugger must have escaped from Franco's Pet Emporium on the second floor. Thing is, he knew that fat old shithead didn't have anything more exotic in that place anymore, not since the baby alligator incident. The only animals suffering in that shop were two old rabbits and a parrot missing its feathers. Besides, Desmond would have heard about it by now.

It didn't matter where it had come from. The bird-thing belonged to him now and that's all that mattered. Desmond closed his special bag and looked up. If Franco wanted to argue otherwise, well, he was welcome to chat to Desmond's fists.

He carried on wheeling his trolley as calm as you like towards the double doors that led to the maintenance areas. He noticed a few more yawning employees slouching about, making their way to their respective shops.

As per usual, not one of them acknowledged him. He was just another piece of the mall, part of the furniture. This was fine by him. Desmond didn't want these drones to meddle in his affairs. They had their world, and Desmond had his world. None of them had a clue of the hidden kingdom lying inches beyond these sparkly walls.

He unlocked the plain grey door and pushed it open, Desmond wheeled the trolley inside and closed the door behind him. Now he felt that he could truly relax, knowing that no bugger would find him in here. This was his place, his sanctuary. Well, it was during his shift. Oh, the other cleaners came here, but only to grab supplies. They didn't venture any further from this storeroom, not like him.

Desmond flicked on the lights, illuminating the rows of blue metal shelves, containing everything the janitors needed to do their jobs. He left the trolley by the door and walked past the clear containers containing the various chemicals they used, past the boxes full of sponges, wipes, and cloths. He moved past the rolls of toilet tissue and the replacement mop heads.

He had no interest in any of that stuff. The other door, the one which led into the maintenance areas, was what had his complete attention. The door that Desmond had locked only twenty minutes ago and now it stood wide open.

"You have got to be having a laugh here," he growled, rushing over to the door. How could this be? There wasn't anybody else in the mall at this time who could have been in here. Even the hired security guards weren't authorised in here. He paused; there was the operations manager but right now, Mrs. Killmore would be making sure that everything was ready for today's trade. She sure as fuck wouldn't be skulking around here.

Desmond held onto the edge of the door trying to stop the shakes. Usually, he wouldn't have cared about it, but his pet was down there. The pet that would be making him a lot of money. This didn't make any sense at all. No matter how many times he went through this, it still came to the simple fact only he and that fat dyke held a key.

"The security cameras!" His mouth dried up. Why hadn't he thought of those? Oh, there were no cameras in the toilets, but there were plenty of them dotted about the mall. One of them must have seen him last night, taking his exotic bird down here. She must have seen him.

Desmond peered around the door expecting to see her standing there with his pet at her feet, her hands planted on her hips, giving him a look that could melt stone. There wasn't anybody there. Hell, the light wasn't even on. Mrs. Killmore wouldn't go down there without turning on the lights. His fingers brushed over the light switch, but he didn't flick the switch. This changed things. It meant that somebody was in there who wasn't allowed. He didn't want to throw any light on the matter, nor did Desmond want to shout out.

His fingers then touched something on the wall that was wet. He brought his digits to his face, frowning at the sight of thick blood dripping from his fingertips. Oh, this changed things all right. Desmond rushed back to his trolley and grabbed the adjustable wrench that he'd tried to fix that dodgy wheel with earlier.

Desmond's suspicious mind had already constructed the whole reason for the open door mystery, a theory which totally fit the facts. He gripped the wrench tightly and hurried over to that door. He flicked on the switch, not giving a crap anymore. It had to be Franco down there, it was obvious now. That slimy dago must have been the one who'd seen him take the bird down here. Of course, he wouldn't have it displayed in his shop. Everyone knew the man was as dodgy as fuck. There's no way that Franco could pay the mall's exorbitant rent through selling a few bags of food. He must have a sideline of selling illegal exotic animals. It all made sense now.

Yeah well, the bird was his now. The cleaner nodded to himself. Nobody stole from Desmond, not unless they enjoyed hospital food. He saw a few more spots of blood along the wall and the floor. He guessed that the bird wasn't too keen on going back either. Unlike Desmond, that Franco obviously hadn't realised just how mean this multi-coloured bird could be.

This blood wasn't going to be Franco's only donation this morning, that's for damn sure. If he could find the thieving bastard that is. Last night's self-assurance that no bugger would find his new pet now hit him right in the face.

How exactly was he going to find the bugger? This place really was a maze of pipes, venting, corridors, and alcoves. He remembered telling Henry that you'd be able to hide a couple of bull elephants down here, as long as they didn't make much noise, of course.

He stopped beside another door which led to a metal ladder to get to the roof. God, he was such an idiot. The first place to check was obviously where he had left his bird last night. Desmond spun around and went back the way he came, until he reached a metal hatch embedded in the corridor wall. As he suspected, the hatch wasn't locked. Then again, Desmond wasn't a hundred percent sure that he had locked it.

The hatch swung open, and he grimaced when his fingers found a couple more spots of wet blood on the edge on the hatch. It looked like his bird hadn't gone without a bit of a fight. "Good for you," he whispered, climbing inside. Desmond crawled along the chute on all fours, continuously cursing at the mess that his hands and knees were sliding through.

It's only when Desmond finally reached the small enclosed room, and gaped at the collection of wet bones and lumps of unidentifiable flesh piled in all four corners, when he believed that perhaps this wasn't one of his brightest ideas. Desmond also believed that maybe this wasn't Franco's doing after all.

Desmond climbed out of the hatch, wiped his hands down the sides of his overalls, and stared at the empty cage in the corner on this slaughterhouse. Oh Lord, had his new pet really caused all this mess? He crouched and surveyed the scattered remains. Now that his mind had settled down, Desmond could now see, that although it looked like somebody had been in here dancing while holding a tin of red paint, the devastation looked worse than it actually was. He reached across and picked up a rat's tail attached to half a body. In fact, there were dozens of gutted rat bodies scattered across the floor.

His pet sure was hungry. There were a few mouse carcasses on the floor as well. No wonder none of the traps had been full. All that remained to check, was where it had gone to, and that large pile of flesh and bones that was right behind him. Desmond decided not to examine that too closely, in case he found something he didn't like.

Desmond had to face facts, his pet could be anywhere by now. There were over a dozen pipes wide enough for it to scurry through in here. Not to mention the hatch that he came through, as well as another pipe on his left that was large enough for even Desmond to squeeze into.

He felt his anger beginning to return. Why the fuck had he left it in here in the first place? He should have taken it home with him last night. Thanks to his incompetence, Desmond had lost out on what could have been a potentially large amount of money.

To make matters even worse, he now had to find another set of overalls to change into. He couldn't exactly walk around Hopeview Mall looking like a murder victim. They'd certainly notice him dressed like this as he pushed that trolley with the fucking squeaky wheel.

"What a mess!"

As he turned to climb back through the hatch, Desmond froze as he heard what sounded like scratching coming from that large tunnel. Could his pet be returning? A smile broke out on his face. Of course it was returning. The bird had been out rat hunting. It was always going to return, after all, this was its little home, its den.

Still grinning, Desmond turned and walked over to the large pipe and stood beside it, getting ready to catch it when it poked its little head through the opening. It must catch them and bring its food here to eat in peace. At least he knew what to feed it now. Desmond looked across at the cage he'd used. It wasn't too badly damaged. He could fix that up while it ate the rat, and then use the food in his special bag to lure it in the fixed-up cage. It sounded like a plan with no faults.

He listened to the sound that of those claws tapping against the inside of that pipe. It sure sounded bigger now, a lot bigger. Desmond found his feet moving back a couple of inches as a large shadow hit the wall above the cage. He heard a noise too, and it sure as fuck wasn't a chirp. This sounded more like the growl of a bear.

His instinct for self-preservation was a lot greater than his greed. Desmond ran back to the hatch just as a feathered muzzle poked through that pipe exit. He almost had a stroke at the sight of what resembled his pet, only much larger. This thing was the size of a pony. Its amber eyes focussed on Desmond. It dropped the severed arm it held in its jaws and leaped out of the pipe.

He shrieked and tried to climb into the hatch, hot piss streaming down both his thighs. Desmond's feet skidded on some gore. He crashed onto the floor, still sobbing and crying. He turned onto his back and watched this brightly coloured nightmarish creature pick up its severed arm, and take it over to the corner, ignoring the fact that he was even there. Desmond sat up, not too sure how he was still alive. That current state wouldn't be permanent if he didn't get a move on. He shuffled backward until his spine hit the wall before slowly standing, keeping his attention on the big bird while it daintily bit off the fingers one by one.

Something in the corner of his eye caught his attention, and Desmond found that he and big bird weren't the only things in this chamber that moved. The pile of bones and flesh in the corner suddenly shifted. Big bird's head lifted at the same time as Desmond turned his head. He groaned in terror when the bones and flesh fell away as what could only be described as a man-shaped animal covered in bright yellow feathers rose.

"I'm dreaming this," said Desmond. "This can't be fucking real."

The bird man lifted its arm and pointed a silver pipe at Big Bird. A high-pitched whistle filled the chamber, and Big Bird fell on its side.

Desmond was already in the hatch crawling away when the high-pitched noise filled the air one more time. He screamed out in utter agony when it felt as though somebody had set every nerve in his body alight.

## CHAPTER FOUR

Leaving the mall for lunch had been the best decision that he had ever made. Jefferson couldn't believe that he hadn't done this before. To think that he'd worked there for almost two years and never set foot outside the building once at lunch. He pushed in the last piece of his Cornish pasty and idly brushed the crumbs off his lap before taking a sip of coffee. The food hadn't been that great, and this coffee was instant, but none of that mattered. For the first time in two years, he was able to enjoy his meal in relative silence, as well as being able to watch those clouds roll across that beautiful blue sky.

"Silence is definitely golden," he whispered, smiling as a startled pigeon flew past the cafe window, almost crashing into a lamp post. "Stupid bird."

The last straw, the one that did break the camel's back and cemented his decision to ditch those losers and leave the mall, happened at morning break when David came out with yet another one of his lies and told everybody at their table that he heard some kid had been taken to hospital because some stray dog had bitten this kid on the leg.

Although it did sound weird, something like this happening wasn't beyond the realms of possibility. What pissed off Jefferson was David's inability not to jump into *bullshit land*. He then leaned across the table, and in some conspiratorial voice, told everybody that this dog was covered in bright blue feathers.

This had to be his best idea yet. He already felt the stress and misery sloughing away. He'd already decided to visit the library tomorrow after grabbing a burger from the Wimpy bar on Needle Road. He'd have gone there today if it hadn't been for that annoying old bloke campaigning for some charity, who accosted him as soon as he left the mall.

Jefferson drained his coffee, stood, and smiled at the pretty waitress who'd served him before leaving the cafe. It was time to return and face the music. With some luck, David would get in a strop on not talk to him for the rest of the day for abandoning them. "I can only hope."

He stopped just outside the shop and watched a parade of soldiers marching past the city hall. Jefferson would have to mention this to Sandy; she had a thing for men in uniform. Especially ones carrying guns. Obviously, he would wait until he was in the company of David before he opened his mouth, just to enjoy the fleeting look of extreme jealousy on his face while Sandy told them how they made her go weak at the knees.

Would Sandy have noticed Jefferson if he had been in uniform? That thought made him smile, considering how close he'd been to joining up. His dad, brother, and two uncles were in the military. Jefferson still remembered his dad's look of disappointment that the old man had tried so hard to hide when Jefferson had told him flatly that he had no intention of getting himself blown up or shot at.

Looking back at his rather rash decision and how his future had panned out, perhaps joining up would have been a better choice. "I should have dragged Sandy out here. She'd love this." The parade had drawn quite a crowd, mostly women. The officer at the front looked so much like his old man it was unreal. Jefferson found himself waving and was a little surprised when the officer winked back at him.

Jefferson sighed when he noticed the city hall clock gently reminding him that if he didn't get his arse in gear, he'd be late for work. He turned around and hurried back towards the shopping centre, while trying to remember what rank three diamonds signified. Bloody hell, his dad would have had a heart attack at his dire lack of knowledge. Come to think of it, David would have a go at him too.

He walked down the pedestrian walkway, passing the two banks, a music shop, and a pizza joint. The closer he got to the mall, the more people there were cluttering up the path.

He turned the corner and stopped dead, staring in disbelief at the metal shutters across the entrance. "What the hell?" No way could the mall be shut at this time. They didn't even pull down the shutters when it did close at eight. There was always somebody in the building.

Shutters or no shutters, he still needed to get in there somehow. Jefferson pushed his way through the gathered crowd, trying to spot anyone else who worked in the mall. He couldn't be the only worker who'd gone out for his lunch. This just didn't feel right.

Jefferson had noticed somebody with whom he'd had prior contact. He groaned at the sight of that charity worker enthusiastically heading towards him. It did cross his mind to turn around and get away before that charity worker reached him. He could always use this opportunity to visit that library, either that or go home. Jefferson couldn't do that, though. His friends were inside and because, like a fool, he'd left his phone in his coat pocket, he couldn't contact them until he'd got home anyway.

"Isn't this a bit weird, buddy? Nobody has a clue what's going on here."

So much for the charity being able to update him. He listened to the dreadlocked youth rattle on about some couple being separated when the shutters came down and how nobody could get close to the shutter because they all went a bit funny. This was unreal. Just because this guy tried to fleece him out of his money, they were now fast friends?

"I think it's a fire drill." The youth assumed the air of authority when two other shoppers gazed in his direction. "Yeah, that's got to be the reason. Give it a few more minutes, and the shutters will go back up."

Jefferson nodded and smiled before pretending to look at his watch. He spun around and lost himself in the crowd, squeezing his way through the throng, and headed for the edge of the walkway where the crowds were thinner.

Where were all the police and the fire engines? He skirted around the crowd, deciding to go around the other side of the building. The emergency services should have already got here by now, if only to reassure the shoppers.

It wasn't a fire drill, that much Jefferson did know. Every staff member was supposed to escort the shoppers out of the building; they sure as hell didn't lock them all in. "This doesn't make any sense," he repeated.

On a brighter note, it looked like all the shops in the town centre were about to receive some much needed custom. The crowd was already dispersing, leaving the charity worker leaning against the wall with only a couple of pigeons for company. He picked up the pace, in case the guy tried to collar him again.

What did that clown mean about people feeling weird when they got too close to the shutters? Did it mean anything, or was that guy making up rubbish so people would listen to him? Jefferson hurried past the huge window displays belonging to Martin's Department Store, still unnerved by the complete lack of explanation to why the mall had just closed itself off from the rest of the town.

There should have been somebody around to explain what was going on. Indigo's Furniture Store had another entrance at the back on the mall. Jefferson would try to get inside through there. He knew there wasn't any shutters installed over those doors. He slowed his pace, and then stopped dead at the sight of another set of metal shutters over the furniture shop entrance.

"No, no way," he said. He and David came through those doors this morning. Had they really installed a set of shutters in just over four hours? Jefferson walked over to them and placed his hand on the metal.

His anxiety melted away. Jefferson loved his job. He had great friends and was really happy with his life. He ought to see this as an unexpected holiday. Why not visit that library? Maybe he'd meet a pretty girl in there?

He snatched his hand off the shutter. "What the fuck was that?" he cried. It felt as though something had just melted the surface of his brain. Jefferson clamped his hand over his mouth, trying not to throw up. His handprint now stained the shutter. Through the shape, he saw what looked like glass. Despite his whole body suggesting otherwise, Jefferson put both hands on the shutter and pressed. Jefferson loved his job. He had great friends, and he was really—

He fell to his knees and bent over. Jefferson slammed his hands on the tiled floor and groaned as nausea slammed through his guts. He managed to open his eyes to find himself in the store's lobby. Holding his hands against his stomach, Jefferson turned his head to find the automatic doors leading outside were wide open. He slowly got to his feet and burped, grimacing as the taste of that pasty filled his mouth.

Two young girls came into view. They stopped opposite him and stared, only they weren't looking at him.

"Oh, it's closed," said the blonde girl.

Her companion swore before she took a lump of pink gum out of her mouth. Jefferson gaped in incredulity as it looked like she was about to give it to him. Instead, she pushed it against the fresh air. He saw the gum flatten out. It just stayed there, defying gravity, while the other girl let out a loud sigh.

"Fuck it, let's go to McDonald's then."

The girls ran over the road, narrowly avoiding a speeding white van, leaving him standing there gazing at that piece of floating gum. He reached for it then stopped. Whatever was there had already made him feel like he'd dropped his guts into a cement mixer. Did he want to go through that again? Jefferson decided it wouldn't be worth the pain.

He turned around and slowly walked into the furniture store.

If it wasn't for his stomach behaving like he'd just spent the past few hours on a roller-coaster, Jefferson would feel pretty chilled. Better than he'd felt for weeks. Even the mall looking closed, or he'd just walked through a metal shutter, or seeing floating gum wasn't dinting this weird high.

"I love my job," he said, strolling through the empty showroom. "I have great friends." He stopped to admire a corner bookcase, thinking it would look great in his bedroom. Jefferson was aware that something was seriously wrong here, that nobody was about, and the coffee table next to him had four deep scratches across the previously polished mahogany surface. There was also the small matter of that lake of blood by the till-point number one. Yet all Jefferson could think about was that he was really happy with his life.

The mall's generic annoying music competed with this store's own choice of classical. He found himself humming to Strauss while admiring a double bed. He was thinking he should still go to the library. Maybe he'll meet a pretty girl in there.

Jefferson looked over at the entrance which led outside the mall, then at the mall concourse behind the till-points, and wiped away hot tears. "I love my job. I have great friends." He dropped to his knees again, and this time, he did empty his guts across the tiles. He fell onto his side and rolled under the bed while thinking that someone had just detonated a grenade between his ears.

He screwed up his eyes, feverishly wishing that this weird nausea would leave him alone. What the hell had just happened to him? His thoughts were trapped in thick glue. His recent memory had separated into fragments, and no matter how hard he tried, they refuse to coalesce. His last reliable image was of sitting in some cafe while watching a pigeon crash into a building, then, pick itself up as if nothing had happened before pecking at the pavement in search of food. Even with his eyes shut, Jefferson could still hear it pecking away.

He snapped open his eyes, realising that the sound wasn't in his head. He looked in confusion at bedsprings a couple of inches from his nose before turning his head to the left. The question as to why he was lying under some bed flew out of his head when he saw some two-legged lizard with a long neck and tail pushing a lump of brown mush with its tiny head through a puddle of vomit.

It jerked its head up, fastened him with a brief stare, and let out a squawk before returning to its previous task. Was that a…? Jefferson couldn't even bring himself to utter the name, but what else could it be? He did know that if David was here, he'd be able to tell him for sure. The lad was almost as obsessed with dinosaurs as he was with toy cars and Star Wars.

He thrust his hand into his pocket and pulled out a chocolate bar that Sandy had given to him at morning break. The rattling had already caught the attention of the little animal. It swallowed the brown lump first, and then slowly approached the bed, with its head bopping up and down. It took effort for him not to smile at its antics. The behaviour reminded Jefferson of the nodding dog that his dad had stuck on the back window of his car.

"You want some of this?" he asked, peeling back the wrapper. "Sure you do, little guy."

It took one more step towards him then stopped, it froze.

"Come on, don't be shy." Jefferson dropped the chocolate and clamped his hand over his mouth, this time to muffle a shocked scream as a huge pair of jaws appeared from nowhere and clamped over the little dinosaur's neck, snapping off the head. He shuffled back when those jaws lowered again and scooped up the rest of the corpse.

Jefferson kept his hand against his mouth, watching as his narrow view revealed some more of this new arrival's body. A pair of thickly muscled legs, covered in dark red feathers, walked past the bed. They stopped beside that pool of vomit for a moment. He heard it gulping down its food before the creature moved over to the till-point. Jefferson found enough courage to move a little closer to the edge of the bed so he could get a better look.

There was no mistaking it, this one definitely shouldn't exist anymore. He vividly recalled David going absolutely ape-shit after watching a certain dinosaur movie set in a park. He went on for weeks, banging on that raptors were feathered like birds. Jefferson telling the lad that it didn't make any difference went through one ear and out of the other.

This was one of David's feathered raptors, just metres from him, in the flesh and hungry for flesh. There was no doubt in him that if he had been on view, that collection of curved teeth would right now be chewing on his bones.

Jefferson poked his head out and watched it jump onto the roof of the showroom car before it ran onto the interior of the department store. He climbed out from under the bed and sat on the mattress. He gripped his knees and shook like a leaf while wondering if he was having some kind of mental breakdown.

"Come on, man. Get a grip on yourself," he said, managing to stand without falling back on the bed. He fought the urge to crawl back underneath the bed. Jefferson waited until he was sure that the monster wasn't going to run back out of that department store before he made his way over to the first till-point. He leaned on the counter and scanned the concourse, looking for any signs of movement. Human movements, that is. He had no fucking desire to run into another one of those carnivorous ostriches without the reassurance of a fucking shotgun in his hands. "What the fuck happened in here?"

Jefferson almost ran back to the bed when he heard a noise coming from directly behind this till-point. It took a second for him to realise that his ears had heard a quiet sob and not the sound of another freaky animal wanting to bite off his head.

He slowly leaned over the edge and clapped eyes upon a blonde-haired woman. Her blue eyes found his. She blinked. "Are you okay, miss?" he asked. It took him a moment to realise that he knew the woman. This was Janine Butler, the store's assistant manager. She was almost unrecognisable under the tear-stained foundation, mascara, and blusher. Seeing someone who took so much effort over her appearance in this state was almost as shocking as finding he'd been dropped onto dinosaur island.

He walked around the edge of the counter and crouched directly in front of her. "Miss, it's okay. That thing's gone now. You're safe."

Janine let out another quiet sob before she launched herself at Jefferson and wrapped her arms around his body. He felt so awkward reciprocating her gesture, but when it became obvious that she was in no rush to let him go, Jefferson put his arms around her too.

"I, I thought I was the only one left," she whispered. "I can't tell you how good it is to find somebody else. That thing, the huge bird-thing. It came in here and ate Mr. Allinson." She swallowed hard. "Oh God, I can still hear the sound of its teeth crunching through his head." The woman looked up. "What's going on?"

He let her go and stood, feeling his face reddening. Jefferson didn't reply, deciding not to tell her that he was as clueless as her. Jefferson helped her up, he also decided that he'd keep the floating gum event to himself as well. "You've seen nobody else, Mrs. Butler?"

She shook her head. "Not since about eleven. It's been a quiet day."

He nodded. This store usually only attracted the browsers. Most of the stuff in here was too expensive. Alan told the gang that he went in here a couple of days ago, when his partner was after a new wardrobe. He still ended up buying a piece online. "What's outside the store? I mean, like people walking past." Jefferson took a couple of steps towards the concourse and stopped when the woman slipped her hand into his.

"Don't, please. Don't leave me."

"I won't leave, you, Mrs. Butler."

"Janine. Call me Janine."

"People, you were about to tell me about other people."

The woman squeezed his hand. "I'm sorry. When that thing did that awful thing to Mr. Allinson, I ducked under here and didn't move." She gazed fearfully around. "Has it gone? I mean, it's not hiding somewhere? The monster does that, you know. I saw a boy about your age rush in here. Just like you did. He must have thought he was safe in here. The monster leaped off the top of a bunk-bed and dragged him out of the shop. Are you sure you're not going to leave me?"

Had she seen David? Oh God, please don't let it be David. "So you haven't tried to leave the shop?"

The woman sighed. "Hiding behind the counter wasn't my first choice. I did try to escape, only somebody must have put the shutters down."

"What shutters? The shop doesn't have any." Jefferson was about to add that is how he got in, then changed his mind. "It must have, otherwise I would be halfway to bleeding China by now. I love my job. I have great friends."

Jefferson's scrambled memory slotted back into place. He remembered placing his two hands on that shutter and finding himself in the store lobby, as well as repeating the same word that the woman had just uttered. Christ, just what the frig was going on in here? "Look, miss. I need to find my friends." He looked over to the exit. "Believe me, there's no shutter over those doors. All you have to do is close your eyes and walk through." He pulled her fingers out of his hand. "Trust me on this. You're safe now. That monster has gone."

She forced her hand back and shook her head. "No, I'm not leaving you, mister. I'm going where you're going."

Jefferson reached into his pocket and pulled out his blue plastic box cutter. He slapped it on the counter. "In that case, we're going to need something to use if that thing comes back, as I think that will be about as useful as a chocolate fireguard."

The woman looked around the under the counter, pulling out plastic bags, and coat hangers. She then straightened her back and placed a craft knife in the palm of his hand. "That belongs to Mr. Allinson."

Jefferson tried not to laugh at the sight of the very same type of craft knife that they sold in his shop. "It's better than nothing, I guess." He pushed out the blade. "Although it is still only one claw versus ten claws and a gobful of teeth. I doubt that dinosaur will be shaking in its boots."

"You mean that's a dinosaur?"

"It isn't a cat, honey." David might not have been talking rubbish about that feathered dog after all. He pushed out the blade before sneaking out of the furniture shop. He crouched beside the pretzel stall and scanned the concourse, looking for signs of movement. The eatery and the group of shops where he and his mates worked were around the corner. To get there, the pair of them had to pass the department store. Right now, Jefferson wasn't that keen on doing so, not after the woman had told him about the bunkbed incident.

He had seen enough wildlife documentaries to recognise an ambush predator when he saw one, and neither of them had been all that quiet. He could see those evil claws whipping out from behind that handbag stand and ripping the woman out of his grip as soon as they passed that shop.

"I don't understand. How can it be a dinosaur? I thought that they all died out millions of years ago."

"Mrs. Butler, do you have any children?"

"Yes. I have two boys a bit younger than you. Why do you ask?"

"What did you used to say to them when they were about five and kept asking you stupid questions?"

"Sorry."

"No, I'm sorry. That was uncalled for." He took a handkerchief out of his back pocket. "Here, you go, Mrs. Butler. I mean, Janine."

She took it out of his hand. "Thank you."

He knew it wasn't the only dinosaur, at least didn't used to be the only one. Meaning, how many more of them were they in the mall? And how many more of them stood between him and his friends? He looked down at the knife in his hand then across at the sporting goods shop opposite him. "Come on, Janine."

"Why, what are we doing?"

"We need to even the odds," he replied, pulling her over to the shop. "We're going to get tooled up."

He hurried past the football shirts and the trainers, not slowing down until he reached the counter. "You'll have to let go of my hand a moment." Jefferson climbed onto the surface and reached for the crossbow attached to the wall.

"It'll be locked. You're going to need the key. You'll need the key for that metal cabinet too. It's where they keep the bolts."

"Great," he muttered. "Just great." He turned around, using his higher elevation to survey the shop. Just like everywhere else, the place looked deserted. He'd already discovered, though, that this didn't mean there wasn't anybody about. Even so, he wasn't about to start shouting for assistance. The woman pushed her body between his feet. She reached over the counter and chuckled.

"This might help."

He jumped down, grinning at the sight of the cricket bat she held. It wasn't one they sold in here. It looked more at home in the hands of some dodgy-looking pub landlord with those metal spikes embedded in the end.

"This belongs to Danny," she said. "Some guy came into his shop a few months ago and pulled this out of a carrier bag. He told the young girl that if she didn't give him all the money in the till then he'd use this on her face. What the idiot didn't know was that Danny had already seen him. The would-be burglar was on the floor and out cold before another threat could come out of his mouth." She handed it to him. "It's not as good as a crossbow, but it's bound to help you more than the original owner."

"I wish Danny was here now," said Jefferson.

Janine took his hand. "I think you're doing just great."

Jefferson didn't think he was doing great at all. Right now, he wanted to drop this stupid bat, run to the toilets, and hide in a cubicle, hoping all this was some weird dream caused by drinking too much coffee. Not like he'd be able to run anywhere alone. Mrs. Butler's vice-like grip on his hand would make sure of that. No matter how much he tried, Jefferson could not picture this woman currently holding his hand, giving him those puppy-dog eyes as that stern-looking, bad-tempered old bat who took great pleasure in giving David a hard time whenever the pair of them walked through her shop.

He smiled back at her. It's odd how she never had a dig at him. David used to say that it's because she thought he and David were riff-raff because they worked at the poor and scumbag store, that they brought down the tone of the whole mall. David used to call her *the chair leg witch*.

Would his mate see Janine as anything but the chair leg witch? Like a potential girlfriend for Jefferson, for example? No, of course not. David saved most of his lust for the untouchable Sandy, with whatever remaining, dished out to any pretty girl who happened to walk into the shop wearing a low cut top.

He came to the conclusion that she must wear that makeup just to look a lot older than she really was, because right now, she did not look a bit like the old crone that he and Davis used to take her for. He reckoned Janine to be in her late thirties, certainly no old than forty. Not that much older than him, give or take a decade.

She really did have a lovely smile and smooth skin.

Oh Christ. What was wrong with him? Why had he suddenly started to think with his loins at a time like this?

"What's on your mind?" she blurted out.

Jefferson reddened again. He felt like he had just been caught with his hand in the cookie jar by his mum. "I was just thinking about those shutters outside your store. I know we can't get out the main entrance, so I was trying to think of another way out of here."

All the blood drained from the woman's face. She even let go of his hand to steady herself. "We don't have any shutters. I've already told you that."

"In that case, why didn't you leave the store when you could?"

Jesus, what the fuck was wrong with him? A single tear ran down the side of her face. He waited for the inevitable mantra of *she loves her job* and *she has lots of friends* to tumble from her mouth. Instead, Jefferson found himself looking at the woman who snarled at David this morning. All traces of her recent femininity had vanished. She spun around and walked out of the shop, leaving him feeling utterly wretched.

Why couldn't she keep his big mouth shut?

"Wait up!" he shouted, running after her. The woman had not gone far. He found her sitting in one of the many seating areas dotted around the mall. All the chairs in this one were green. "Look, I'm sorry, Janine. I shouldn't have snapped at you, it's just…" his words trailed off when he realised that the woman wasn't taking the least bit of noticed in what he said. Her gaze was fixed of the group of dark brown, armoured dinosaurs munching their way through the contents of the fruit and veg in the mini-market.

"Look at them," she said. Her tears had gone; she now looked almost blissfully happy.

"Janine?"

She turned her head and smiled. He couldn't help himself. Jefferson smiled back and took her hand when she offered it.

"Come on." She stood and pulled him into the shop.

"Are you sure this is a good idea? I mean. They're not exactly small."

"Don't be a baby. They are so beautiful!" Janine walked straight up to the first one. She grabbed an apple and held it under the creature's muzzle. Incredibly, it took the fruit straight out of her hand.

He was a little relieved to find it hadn't chomped off any of her fingers too. The woman gave it another apple before she reached out, grabbed Jefferson's arm, and pulled him over. "Go on, pet its head. Look at them, Jefferson. Look how beautiful they are."

"I wish David was here. He'd be able to tell us what they are. I mean, your new pals look like a Brontosaurus, but even I know they're supposed to be a lot bigger than these are, Janine."

"I don't care what they are. I think they're gorgeous." She picked up another apple. "Aren't you a hungry little thing? I love their colours."

"They look like giant bees." The woman chuckled. "Janine, I don't want to sound rude here, but we're supposed to be looking for the others."

"I know. Just one more apple first." She picked up a golden delicious and twisted off the stem. "You do know that we're perfectly safe here in here, David." She placed the apple in her hand. "Safe from that monster, I mean."

Jefferson nodded. He waited for her new friend to take the apple before he gently pulled the woman out of the store, seriously wondering if she was aware of the danger they were both still in. He tried to keep his temper in check and not to tell the woman that this wasn't a fucking petting zoo. All the other shoppers and staff were still missing. If any of them had run into the monster from the furniture shop, then they'd be in bits. It was that simple.

"Come on, we'd best get a move on while that other thing is still behind us." He turned around to make sure that none of those stripy dinosaurs had decided to follow them. Hell, if that thing did come down this way, those poor buggers wouldn't stand a chance. Still, while it was busy eating them, it meant it wouldn't be chasing him and the woman.

Jefferson pulled her across the concourse until he reached the mall corner. He flattened his back against the glass storefront, breathing in the fumes of fresh-brewed coffee drifting out of the open door. There was another more unpleasant smell mixed in with the roasting coffee beans. A taint which had already assaulted his nose when that large predator slaughtered the smaller one.

He squeezed her hand tightly, shut his eyes, and pressed the back of his head against the glass trying to calm himself down. He told himself that it was just another dinosaur corpse lying between those tables and not some headless teenage barista or a waitress with her steaming guts spread across the tiled floor.

"Are you okay, honey?"

He wanted to tell her that he was far from all right, that all he wanted to do was to find his friends and get the hell out of here. He also wanted to tell Janine that his name was Jefferson and not *honey*. "Yeah, I'm fine. Just a bit tired, that's all." Jefferson pulled the woman a little closer to his side and breathed in her perfume, hoping it would mask that sour stench of death.

"I can't hear anything apart from the mall music." He gazed into her eyes. "Please, stay close to me and watch my back. I'm Jefferson, by the way."

She smiled back at him. "I already know your name." She leaned in and gently kissed him. "Don't worry, I'll watch your back."

Jefferson peered around the corner.

"What can you see?"

"Oh no!" he gasped.

## CHAPTER FIVE

His sodden shoes splashed through the shallow pools of black water as Franco raced down the narrow passageway. The man's legs cramped as the burning muscles screamed at him to stop. Every gasping breath that his blow-torched lungs took in felt like his last, and yet he refused to give up.

Thick blood streamed down both his upper arms where the occasional jutting-out nails ripped through his sweat-soaked skin as Franco ran past, but he hardly felt the pain. Nothing was going to get him to stop. Not until he was sure he was safe. Not until Franco had reached the old door which led into the sewer.

"They thought they'd caught me. Well, I showed them. Sure I did. Fuck Killmore. Fuck those stupid shoppers, and most of all, fuck whatever those things were." Franco slowed, just enough for him to get enough air inside his body and to glance back the way he came. None of those things were following him. Of course they weren't. They were as thick as frozen shit, the lot of them.

He broke into a relieved grin when the old door came into view. He'd done it, nobody or nothing could outwit old Franco on his patch. No matter what the creepy janitor thought, this was his patch.

It was a little odd how he'd not seen that dirty old man on the upper levels when they were all being herded together. Then again, knowing that cowardly piece of frozen shit, as soon as the fucking lizard birdmen showed, Desmond would have disappeared faster than the food the janitor stuffed down the front of his pants.

He saw Killmore though, swanning through that crowd of bubble-headed morons giving out all these annoying reassuring platitudes. Thing is, Franco knew she was just going through the motions, that her words weren't having any effect on the assembled shoppers and staff. They weren't working because those lizard birdmen had already done something to them first. They didn't catch him, though. No way was he going to march to any pied piper.

Franco's bones had been itching like a bastard all night. He always got like this before one of his deals were close to finalising. He sighed heavily, deciding that they weren't chasing him after all. He sat down on an overturned metal box and wiped his brow. Franco had been that close to saying *fuck it* and staying in bed. It's not like he really needed to open the pet shop. No bugger came in there anyway, not to buy stuff. He'd only be spending the day getting stressed out at the sight of the bubble heads coming in all the time and disturbing his rabbits and guinea pigs by ignoring his signs and tapping on the glass.

The kids were the worst. If he had his way, Franco would have every one of the little fuckers euthanized. It was the only way to deal with them in his book. Granted, he knew his temper had gotten worse over the past couple of days. It wouldn't get any better until the deal had gone down.

Not all of his animals came through the proper channels. Some of his more expensive clients preferred an animal either endangered or illegal, and he knew enough contacts who could supply him with either.

The ultimate irony of his little side-line is that he would have made a bastard fortune if he'd been able to get to some of those nasty little critters that he had noticed running between the legs of the lizard birdmen.

Franco licked his fingers and gently wiped off some of the dried blood on his arm while trying to make some sense in what had been a thoroughly strange and fucked-up morning. His first thought at the sight of those man-shaped creatures, covered from head to foot in a soft yellow down striding along the upper balcony, was that the mall had put on some kind of stupid festival again. His opinion soon changed when a security guard ran at one of them, only for his intended target to pull out a short pipe. Within seconds, the uniformed fool stopped dead in his tracks. Even from his position behind his till, Franco could see this man develop a huge grin over his face before turning around, walking up to the thick glass barrier, and throwing himself over the edge. Right at that moment, when the bone-smashing noise reached his ears, he realised that it didn't matter about the reason for their sudden appearance. All that mattered was for Franco not to end up as a concourse pizza. His own survival took precedence over everything else, and that included the two young girls who'd been sighing over his two floppy-eared grey rabbits.

He remembered ducking behind the counter and waiting for the two brats to hear the fun and games outside. Franco's mum did not raise any fools. He knew just how important it was for those kids to believe that he had *fucked out* of the shop as well. Kids were gobby. They seemed to get off on grassing over people.

Just like the stupid rabbits they had been cooing over, the two girls quickly forgot their object of fascination as soon as they heard the excitable noises coming from outside. Franco watched them from behind his hiding place, silently urging them to hurry up and get the fuck out of his shop before those yellow-feathered bastards reached his shopfront. They'd only have to look through to glass to see his fat arse cowering under his cash register.

Franco allowed a slight smile of relief to ghost over his face when they finally buggered off. He ran around to the other side and hurried straight for the rabbit cages. He glanced around just once, before he ran his fingers along the side of the wooden cage until reaching a groove in the grain. Digging in his fingernails, he pulled out a block of wood the same size as a postage stamp, revealing a metal keyhole. Franco pulled out his wallet, took out a small silver key, and pushed it in before turning it. He heard a quiet click before a door-shaped panel swung open.

After replacing the block back into the slot, Franco disappeared behind the panel. As the false door closed behind him, the sounds of those two girls shrieking reached him. Franco guessed that their mothers did raise fools. If he had been in their shoes, Franco wouldn't have gone out there, no chance. He'd have thrown himself under the shelving and pulling down some dog food bags. As far as he was concerned, it served them right for being so bloody nosy.

Franco finished cleaning his left shoulder and got to work on his other one. It had only been about an hour since he'd escaped from the carnage on the upper floor, and yet it felt like a full day had passed. He closed his eyes, wincing as the pain from the shoulder wounds finally caught up with him.

He had waited for a few minutes before leaving his beloved pet shop. His professional curiosity piqued to the maximum at the thought of some new life-form in his proximity. Now that he felt safe, Franco could at least indulge his inquisitive nature, even if it was for just a minute or two.

His heart rate went into fucking overdrive when two of them ambled into his shop. Oh Jesus, Mary, Joseph and all the stable animals! They weren't birdmen at all. The two of them reminded Franco of upright bearded dragons without any tails, but only in a superficial way. He knew without a doubt that these creatures were intelligent, and deadly. The claws on their hands and feet proved that. They both moved like a cross between a stalking cat and an excitable fat kid in a cake shop, especially when they spotted his caged animals.

He jumped back, almost crashing into the cages which he stored his illegal animals, when they ran up to the two rabbits. God, they were fast! Thankfully, this area was completely soundproofed. So even if he had made any noise, they wouldn't have heard him, he hoped.

These new creatures were hunters though, so who knows what other senses they used to find their prey. Franco decided, while one of them was trying to figure out how to open the rabbit cage, that enough was enough. He left them to it and left the hidden room by way of a hatch, set into the wall behind him.

Franco stood and examined the holes and grazes on his shoulders before he made his way towards the next door. He so wished he had grabbed his phone before running. Like the fool that he was, he had left the bloody thing beside the cash register. It would have been nice to have snapped a few pictures before leaving the mall.

Then again, maybe not. Any hesitation on his part might have meant that poor Franco here could have ended up back in there, along with all those other bubble heads, all waiting like stupid cattle at the gates to an abattoir, waiting for their imminent slaughter.

The feathered iguanas had pulled out ten people from the assembled crowd. Franco did note that each person selected was either from a different ethnic background or a different age. The last one was a little girl that one of them pulled out of a green pushchair. Just like that security guard, none of those shoppers had shown any distress at being herded into the middle of the concourse between a craft shop and a music store. From his hiding place behind a supporting pillar in the jewellers next to his pet shop, Franco witnessed a sight which even eclipsed the appearance of these terrible invaders. Franco had given their arrival some thought whilst squeezing his body between the outer wall and the false partitions. He came to the conclusion that the Earth had been invaded by aliens. It was either that or some kids had cooked them up with those chemistry sets that had been on sale in that shop opposite him over Christmas.

He saw dinosaurs, honest to God *dinosaurs*. They weren't the size of that T-rex, or the one with three horns, but they were dinosaurs all the same. He counted eight animals, about the length of a pony, with their heads coming up to his shoulder. These looked just like the other dinosaurs from that kiddie movie set in a park. Velociraptor, that's what they were called. Only in the movie, those nasty bastards weren't covered in fucking canary feathers.

Like a bomb going off in his head, Franco then understood exactly what he was seeing here. He watched those iguana men guiding the raptors in a single file through the crowds. Like the humans, those animals were acting just like sheep. Franco would have loved to know how they were able to control both the humans and the dinosaurs right now, though. He pushed that question to the back of his head, just happy that he'd worked out exactly what they were.

The similarity between the raptors and these upright feathered lizards were plain for all to see. They were evolutionary relatives; it was like comparing him to a monkey. Ha! So much for his alien theory.

The raptors and the small assembled humans were now rubbing shoulders in the middle of the concourse, separate from all the other shoppers. One lizard man walked around the perimeter and placed cylindrical objects around the two species before returning to join its companions.

The air around the group shimmered before what appeared to be a glass dome formed around the group, then whatever spell the iguana men had over the group vanished. The slaughter that followed burned into Franco's retinas as those hooked claws sliced through human skin and muscle.

This energy field might have stopped all that deluge of blood from escaping, but it didn't stop those bird-like screeching and the short-lived screams from reaching his ears. Franco looked away when the interior of the dome turned completely red.

The squawks stopped a few seconds later, so he guessed that the feathered men had used those pipes on the raptors again. When he looked back, he found to his horror that the energy field was no longer on. The raptors were busy guzzling down the remaining pieces of meat. What made Franco's heart miss a bit was the feather men were all looking directly at where he was hiding. Two of them raised their pipes.

Franco reached the door which led into the town's sewer network. He needed to work out what to do once he reached home. He hadn't given his future much thought until now. It's obvious that he couldn't contact the police. Those bastards could all suck on a plate full of frozen shit. No way he could allow the authorities to get in on this one.

He had a couple of shotguns hidden under his floorboards, and with the help of a couple of trusted buddies who lived close by, Franco reckoned he'd be able to bag a couple of those raptors and get them out without anyone realising. Hell, he might even be able to grab a birdman as well. He nodded to himself, yeah *why the fuck not*? After the stress they had put him through, he deserved some kind of recompense. It was only fair. Also, he so wanted to lay his hands on one of those pipes. The fun he could have with a device like that just boggled the mind.

He wasn't exactly sure how to explain his adventure to Danny and his older brother, but Franco should be able to come up with something plausible enough for the lads to follow him back into the sewers.

Franco placed his hand upon the door handle. His thoughts of coming back just fizzled away. He smiled and let out a quiet giggle. Franco loved his job. He had some great friends, and he knew he shouldn't be down here, not when the mall was about to get busy.

The pet shop owner slowly turned out and walked back the way he came still grinning, and why shouldn't he grin. After all, he loved his job. He had such terrific friends. In fact, he could see two of them right now skittering towards him, both of them holding a length of metal pipe.

## CHAPTER SIX

Opening his eyes had to rank as one of the worst decisions that Desmond had ever made. He was still in that dirty chamber with the fluffy dinosaur still in that corner, glaring at him with those hateful green eyes. Since he'd fallen into dreamland, the dinosaur must have gone out for another takeaway as it now had a naked human torso next to those blood-stained claws.

"Come near me, you fluffy fucker, and I'll bite you on the snout."

The raptor growled at him before it lowered its head and sank its teeth into its meal, while still glaring at Desmond.

"I would not recommend pursuing an agenda of aggression. You are a prey animal, act like it. I do not have enough power to keep this device at running at full capacity."

Desmond stifled a scream. He'd totally forgotten about seeing that feathered man rising up from under all those bones and lumps of flesh. Only it no longer looked like some giant bird. He frowned, wondering how his best mate had managed to find him. Not that he was going to complain about good old Henry Wild risking life and limb to come to his rescue. No way. Neither was he going to ask why Mr. Dinosaur here hadn't bitten off Henry's face either. "Oh man, I'm so glad to see you."

Henry turned his head yet he didn't return Desmond's smile. He felt fingers of ice run up and down his spine when Henry told him to stop talking, yet the man's mouth never moved. He felt like he was looking at a showroom dummy.

He leaned closer and squinted his eyes. It wasn't his mate standing there at all. This was some kind of illusion. Under the facade of flesh and janitor's uniform, Desmond could make out yellow feathers. It was like staring at a projection. The only thing stopping him from diving at this monstrosity was the raptor's posture. He got the feeling that any sudden moves on his party would result in swapping that gnawed torso for his body. "What the fuck are you? More to the point, what happened to my friend?"

"Understanding danger must have been a trait bred out of you, or perhaps having nothing to fear has necessitated this obvious survival ability into a redundant genetic sequence? As you cannot function without this desire for information, I shall furnish your appetite."

Desmond did his best to digest what it had said to him. A difficult task with him only understanding one word in ten.

"I scanned your companion's dimensions into my Image Resonator before I ate him. As for what I am, well, that is one question that I too posed upon escaping from my incarnation. You are a fascinating species, my new slave. You are weak, primitive, and your intelligence levels are not far removed from the vermin ancestors. Still, despite all these setbacks, you have broken through the confines which binds every other living organism into place. I would be suitably impressed if you had reached this stage of development without my help."

He still had little clue to what this thing was banging on about, nor did he care. Desmond just wanted to get out of here and go home. He didn't feel very well at all. Desmond then realised what this fucker had just said. "Wait on, did you say you ate my friend?" His sudden loud noise had startled the dinosaur, but right now, Desmond couldn't give a shit. "You evil fucking scumbag. You utter bastard. He was the only friend I had!"

The image of his now dead friend pointed to what looked like a length of copper pipe at his head. Desmond remembered what happen to him last time and bit on the inside of his cheek. He sat back down and took a deep breath. He got the feeling that if he was put back to sleep again, he wouldn't be waking up ever again.

"An interesting reaction, but not entirely unexpected." The image walked through the pile of bones and sludge, stopping when it reached Desmond's feet. "You live still because I wish it, Desmond. Of course, if you do want to truly become a prey, raise your paw now. I shall deactivate the pacifier which is stopping my ancient ancestor from eating you, and she so desires this. If you did choose this option, your death will be painful. You see, because you angered her, she will start by eating your feet. You will cry out in complete agony as her teeth sink into your tender flesh. Is this what you want?"

Desmond shook his head so much he gave himself a headache. "Oh please, no, don't do that. I don't want that to happen. Please don't let her eat me!" He groaned, partly in disgust, when his bladder gave out. The smell of his urine filled his nose. Desmond began to weep. "I'm sorry," he sniffled. "Fuck Harry. He wasn't that much of a friend anyway."

"I have viewed your world through a primitive imaging and communication device. I am sure that the individuals who were with me will have performed a similar action. Despite our faith difference, they would have reached the same conclusion as I did."

Desmond wiped his eyes. "Is this going to upset me?"

"If you were not such an instinctively duplicitous and cunning specimen, then I would believe the news would cause you some upset. For you see, your species is not that far removed from your rodent beginnings. If they were the apex lifeform upon this planet, then they too would breed without regard. They too would damage their environment without concern, and they would continue upon this course until they wiped themselves out."

The image of his now dead friend walked over to the dinosaur and stroked it on the top of the heads like it was some kind of giant kitten.

Desmond still wondered if all of this was an intense dream. "There are more like you?"

"Yes, thirty-one females, thirty of them still within breeding age, and eighteen males. Enough to rebuild our civilization... Once they have exterminated every single one of your species first. Your species perhaps has two more lunar cycles to enjoy their existence."

The image's face then smiled. After getting used to its fixed expression, the sudden change scared Desmond almost as much as its prediction of Armageddon. "You should not allow this to upset you, my new slave. After all, I too am in this position. Unlike those Godless deviants, I do not have another member of my own species who will mate with me. Not that this problem overly concerns me."

Conflicting emotions ran through Desmond's mind. Deep down, he knew that getting out of here and warning as many people as possible should be his only consideration. It didn't matter whether this thing and his pals were capable of murdering billions of people; this guy here certainly believed it. What stopped him from doing exactly that, apart from not wanting that dino to eat his feet, was that Desmond didn't like other people. In fact, the way he saw it, life would be a lot easier without having other people telling him what to do every single day. "Wait a minute, mister."

The image sat down opposite the dinosaur and casually tore off a piece of that torso. "Your colloquialism fascinates me almost as much as your species. Am I to deduce that you wish to ask a question?"

"Okay, so I'm now your new slave. I'm cool with that. Fuck, I've been a slave all my working life, as well as in the forces, so it's not much of a problem. I take that you don't want to kill us all then?"

The image of his old friend disappeared, and the feathered creature reappeared. Desmond quietly congratulated himself for not shitting his pants when this happened. He also praised his nerves when it bit into the chunk of human meat.

"Not every human. Just enough to stop you vermin from becoming a problem for the foreseeable future. The remainder of your species shall be neutered, genetically altered to curb some of that latent aggression and confined to a nature reserve."

"But they'll still look the same? I mean, it's not like they'll look like freaks or anything?" Desmond carefully got back on his feet. "It's just. Well, I know you don't have any chicks and that's a shame, it really is. I was just, well…"

"You crave a mate?"

He thought of that hot chick who worked in the nail bar. "Yeah, a mate. That would be pretty cool." He guessed the chick wouldn't be all that happy about it, but that wouldn't matter. Lizardman would see to that. "So when do we start?"

## CHAPTER SEVEN

The dark interior promised only danger. That much, Jefferson did know. He pressed his nose against the toy shop's glass, trying to see anything remotely human inside. All he saw were eyes belonging to another one of those things which caused all that mayhem in the furniture shop. Thankfully, this one was only the size of a large cat. Even so, he wasn't going to take any chances.

Not that the miniature murderer had that much interest in the two humans outside the shop. Perched on the top shelves amongst the action figures, building blocks, dolls, and board games were dozens of weird-looking flying animals. They looked like bats, only these bastards had a long beak like a pelican and a bony crest on the top of their heads.

The miniature murderer ran from aisle to aisle, leaping at the shelves whenever one of them took to the air. Jefferson had seen birds in his garden behaving in the same manner whenever Alistair, his neighbour's tom cat, sneaked under the fence. He left them to it. There wasn't any death smell drifting out from the interior, so he assumed that Alan, and whoever else was in there, had escaped. He stopped beside Tailor's Beauty Parlour. Unlike the pet shop, the harsh white light still illuminated the interior. Jefferson tried not to let his disappointment show at the sight of the empty shop. Christ, was he still expecting to see the very lovely Sandy sitting on that bright purple chair in front of that black table, waiting for her next customer?

"I don't think there's anybody in there, Jefferson."

He nodded. "I guess not." Sandy stuck her tongue out at him yesterday. It had been at about this time as well. He, of course, did the same back. This went on for a few more seconds, until Jefferson noticed Alan's disapproving gaze in the toy shop window. Jefferson gave him a silent raspberry before he turned around and slouched back to his shop.

He'd give his right arm for everything to go back to how it was, with him being bored and frustrated with his life, and David lusting after Sandy and... He paused and gazed at Janine, still clinging on to his hand. Maybe not everything.

"I don't think that your friends are in there, Jefferson."

He slowly turned, leaned forward, and gently kissed the woman. She eagerly responded, holding him tightly against her body. Jefferson peeled his lips away. He grinned. Janine then pushed out his tongue. "Sorry, I'm not sure why I did that."

"Maybe it's because you could?" Janine sighed softly. "Because you're as terrified as I am, and you think that the chances of both of us getting out of the fucking mall in one piece are pretty slim?"

He wiped away her tears. "We haven't done too badly so far, Janine. Hell, we haven't even used the bat just yet." He kissed her again. "Don't forget, it isn't over until the fat lady sings."

A quiet sob escaped from her mouth. "I hope that isn't a reference to me, young man."

Jefferson shook his head. "Don't be silly, Janine. You're in great shape, considering."

"Considering what? Were you going to say considering my age?"

He laughed. "Both Sandy and Alan used to tell me that the best way to distract a woman was to mention her age." Jefferson gently stroked her cheeks. He wondered if the weird feelings now blasting through his system were due to him falling for this woman or the constant terror of his situation had finally started to make him go a little mental.

"I want you to kiss me again, Jefferson. In fact, I want that more than anything." She hung her head. "But I think we should find your friends first."

"There's only my shop to check. Oh, and the eatery."

She pulled him away from the window and crossed the concourse, heading for the large collection of tables on the other side. Jefferson spent most of his free work time in here, they all did. They alternated through the eight food stalls situated around the U-shaped wall, choosing one per day. Jefferson always opted for the Chinese Express nine-item portion containers.

Jefferson froze. He pulled the woman back and ducked when he spotted three fast-moving shadows in the corner of the eatery. Janine tapped him on the shoulder, then pointed to the cricket bat.

Her intention was very clear. He slowly nodded before standing again. Whatever they were, he didn't believe they would be too much of a threat. The shadows were too small to belong to that beast from the furniture shop. Could it be more of those miniature murderers? That bugger was fast, and it wasn't exactly harmless.

Maybe he ought to bypass the eatery and head for his discount store. Jefferson couldn't remove the image of him storming in there, bat raised above his head, while several more of those things leaped onto Janine. He looked at the woman, not sure what to do. One thing was clear though, he didn't want to be alone again.

The sound of a familiar male voice shouting and swearing totally changed his mind. "That's David!" he gasped. He raced into the eatery, skidding to a sudden stop when he saw literally dozens of the small dinosaurs he first saw from under the bed. They were all crowded around the fried chicken counter, jumping up and down, trying to get to his friend, David.

The lad had one foot on the cash register and the other one stuck inside the glass, which still contained a couple of cream buns. He held a metal fry basket in his left hand, swiping at any of the little dinosaurs that managed to get their claws onto the edge of the counter.

Jefferson turned around, intending to tell Janine to climb onto a table but she was already there, gripping the craft knife.

With her reasonably safe, Jefferson turned his attention to helping David. He gripped the handle tightly, swung it over his shoulder, and smacked the nearest dinosaur with the business end. The impact launched the little animal across the room where it smacked into the front of the iced slushy machine on the burger store counter.

Two other dinosaurs darted out of the way when he tried to hit them. They ducked their heads and squawked at Jefferson before they turned around and raced over to the sandwich shop. They leaped onto the counter and disappeared over the edge. Jefferson waved the bat in the air and jumped up and down. He didn't really want to hit any more of them. Three more darted away leaving only one. It was either stone deaf or just didn't care. It only moved when David jumped backwards and slammed his wire basket on the counter, narrowly missing the creature by inches. It took the hint and ran away.

"You okay, man?"

David dropped the metal basket and frantically ran his fingers up and down both his arms.

"What the hell are you doing?"

"Looking for bites." He stopped and gave Jefferson a huge smile. "God, I can't tell you how happy I am to see your ugly mug. You took a big frigging risk, though." He leaned across and pulled Jefferson towards the counter. "Take a gander at this poor sod."

Jefferson looked over the counter and immediately wished he hadn't. He saw a bloated body sprawled across the tiles. If it hadn't been for the lad's nametag, Jefferson wouldn't have had a clue to the body's identity. The flesh beneath the boy's uniform strained against the material. His exposed flesh had swollen like a balloon. "Oh God, that's disgusting." Jefferson took a deep breath and said a silent prayer for the poor boy. "What happened to him?" He didn't know Simon that well, only enough to exchange nods in passing. A split stretching from his wrist up to Simon's elbow had opened, and thick glutinous blood-streaked yellow pus bubbled over the edges.

"One bite, mate. That's all it took. Simon was on the counter with me. We were trying to get over to the main entrance to see if we could get those shutters up, then those dinosaurs appeared. The next thing I knew, balloon boy down there was on the floor, doing this jerky dance."

Janine had climbed off the table and returned to his side. Jefferson turned away from the dead boy and watched David's eyes widen when the woman interlinked her fingers with his, but he kept quiet about this unexpected turn of events. Jefferson guessed that David's quiet and serious friend was still capable of surprising him after all. Then again, maybe David just had too much going through that brain of his to actually care; after all, for his mate, this must be like winning the lottery, it was a dream come true. David must think that all his birthdays had come at once.

It might also explain his casual approach to Simon's death. It's almost as if David was describing something as banal as spotting roadkill or noticing that the fries on his plate had gone cold. He looked at Janine, wondering if she had seen this. She didn't seem that bothered over the fact that only that counter separated her from some swollen corpse. Maybe the shock of their situation played a large part in how David was behaving, how that all were behaving.

"I don't get this, Jeffdude. I mean, the dinosaur you splatted was a *Coelophysis*. Nice shot, by the way."

Jefferson felt himself zoning out already. He just knew David was about to launch into one of his speeches.

"You see, the time-frame is all out of whack. The *Coelophysis* went extinct in the early Jurassic, yet all the others that I've seen are from the late Cretaceous. The sauropods—"

"The what?" interrupted Jefferson.

"Fuck's sake. The stripy dinosaurs. I've also seen a bunch of Pteranodons, a couple of small raptors, as well as a small Ankylosaur. That's something else that's done my head in. I mean, none of them are any larger than an average human. Good thing too, cos I tell you if an Allosaur or a Spinosaur or a *Carchodontosaurus* came galloping down the middle of the mall, I'd proper shit myself."

This was just unreal. Jefferson stared in disbelief at the boy's flushed face, seriously wondering if the true reality of their dire situation had actually sunk into that thick head of his yet.

"Will you shut the fuck up?" Jefferson let go of Janine, dropped the bat, and wrapped his arms around David. "You're such an annoying nerdy bastard, and I can't tell you how much I've missed you." He let him go and held David at arm's length. "What about the others, have you seen anything of Alan or Sandy?"

He shook his head. "Apart from Simon, you two are the first people I've seen in ages." He grinned. "Thanks, by the way. I'm happy to see you as well." David gazed at the woman. "Hello there, Mrs. Butler. Love the new look."

Janine smiled back at him. "Cheeky little sod."

"So come on, man. What happened here?"

David shrugged. "To be honest, there isn't that much to tell. You know that Mr. Hussain left for that meeting?"

Jefferson nodded.

"Well, once he'd had buggered off, and while you were in the back, I took it upon myself to take a breather in the toilet. Gloria said she'd cover for me."

"I did wonder where you had sneaked off to."

"Anyway, there I was—"

"Playing Candy Buster on your phone."

"Maybe. Well, the Wi-Fi just went off. I couldn't even log into mobile data. Hell, I couldn't get anything out of this piece of shit phone. I left the toilets and found the mall was now almost deserted. There were a few people around, but they were all either waiting by the lift doors or pushing through those double doors over there. It was well weird. They all had this kind of odd smile plastered across their faces as well."

Jefferson thought he knew the reason for that smile. It had to have something to do with whatever was around the shutters, real or pretend one.

"I even tried a couple of the fire doors as well."

He wanted to slap himself. Why hadn't he thought of those? Janine let out a quiet moan. Jefferson guessed that one slipped her by as well.

"The first time I touched the metal bar, I got this, well, weird thought going around my bonce, Jeffdude. I mean, really well weird. Can you believe that I actually thought that I enjoyed working at that shitty discount store? I mean, me, for fuck's sake? Anyway, I tried again, this time with some gloves, same thing happened." He shook his head. "And that's when I started to see the dinosaurs. Jeffdude, I think we may be in a bit of trouble here."

Janine laughed. "That's the first sensible thing you have said."

Jefferson looked up, he saw the reflection of himself and Janine holding hands, while David wouldn't stop plucking at his trouser pockets. He only did that when he was nervous, and he didn't think it was just because a member of the opposite sex was talking to him. What concerned him was what exactly was above that mirrored mosaic? It's the only place where the shoppers and the remaining staff could have gone, and from David's description of the events he saw, they weren't exactly fleeing from any dinosaurs.

"I think we've gone back in time," murmured David.

He looked straight at Jefferson and saw the terror in his mate's face. David really did believe this. Jefferson's stomach rolled, and thought that perhaps his mate hadn't thought that he'd found himself in paradise after all.

"It fits with the energy shield around the shopping mall, it obviously fits with the dinosaurs. As for the reason why there's no large ones, my guess is that the hole inside is only big enough to allow the smaller ones inside."

Jefferson nodded. "Is that your final answer or do you want to phone a friend? Oh wait, you can't cos your phone doesn't work. David, you dork. There isn't any prehistoric jungle beyond those walls, just our shitty town. Where do you think I went at lunchtime? I got back in through the furniture store." He squeezed the woman's hand. "It's how I rescued Janine." Jefferson grinned like an idiot when she smiled at him. He decided to leave out the bit where he threw up and hid under that bed. He picked up the cricket bat, noting the spots of blood on the end. He rested it on his shoulder. He had the girl, he had a weapon, he had his trusty sidekick, all was well.

"Are you going to stop smiling, Jeffdude? You look like you've been snorting coke, or in your case, frigging tea leaves. Look, if we can get out, then let's do it. We need the police. No, fuck them. We need the army and lots and lots of guns."

"Wait on, no. What about Alan and Sandy, man? We can't leave them in here."

"What other choice do we have? I mean. We're not fucking superheroes. There's me, some woman, and a guy with a cricket bat against some of the most efficient killers ever to walk the Earth. It doesn't take a genius to see that we're fucked if we stay."

David's fidgeting grew worse, that wasn't his only concern either. Janine was shaking, really shaking, like she was about to have a fit.

"Oh, and let's not forget the one obvious flaw in this!" he yelled. "It's still fucking time travel, and if we haven't gone back, then someone or something has come here!" He grabbed the front of Jefferson's shirt. "And they're still here, waiting for us on the next fucking level."

Jefferson felt the woman's legs go. It took most of his strength to stop Janine from smashing the back of her head on the floor tiles. He spun to face her, grabbed Janine's other arm, and eased her down on the floor. David had quietened down, but Jefferson could still hear the lad rattling on in the background. "For the love of God, will you shut your gob for a second?"

He slipped out of his jacket, scrunched it up and placed it under her head, and stroked the back of her hand with his forefinger. Jefferson didn't have a clue what else to do.

"My sister has epilepsy, you know," said David. "Don't worry. Your new girlfriend will be out of it soon. You just need to make sure she doesn't swallow her tongue. Tip her head to the side. She'll probably want a drink once she's done. That's what our Debbie asks for."

The woman tilted her head towards Jefferson and slowly opened her eyes.

"Are you all right?"

"I think so." She suddenly gulped down a mouthful of air. "Oh God. That was bloody horrible. It felt like my eyes were going to explode and all my internal organs were on fire."

Jefferson looked towards David, and then switched his gaze back to Janine. He never believed in coincidences, and Janine feeling like shit all of a sudden fit right into the category. She wasn't faking it, that much he did know. "Okay, David. Let's go with your ridiculous bollocks idea of some time travelling thingies are hell-bent on stopping us from escaping. I mean, who'd be daft enough to stick around once they unleash their pet dinos? Apart from you that is, but you're a bit of a prat. I mean normal people."

"Dunno, I guess it depends on their tech level."

"For crying out loud, David, they have time travel. How more advanced do you want?"

"I'd use an energy shield. Yeah, that's what I'd do."

This was getting him nowhere. So much for David being the crown king of geek. "I was thinking of some kind of science fiction gas that makes people want to stay inside. It fucks with people's heads when they the opportunity to get out arises."

"Yeah, sure, seems reasonable. It won't be called that though, cos your name is lame."

"Doesn't fucking matter about the name, man." Jefferson helped Janine into a sitting position. "You don't want to go back to the furniture shop, honey."

She shook her head. "Oh God, you must think me a complete fool. No, I don't want to go back there. Most of all, Jefferson. I don't want you to leave me."

"I'm not going to leave you. I promise." He grabbed the cricket bat by the middle and offered the handle to David. "Here you go, buddy. You might need to hang on to this. If you do manage to make it outside, can you please be quick with the rescue teams? Oh, and make sure they bring some heavy artillery."

David frantically shook his head. For a couple of seconds, Jefferson though he was going to have to look after two epileptics.

"Come on, guys. I don't want to leave you behind, but it makes sense to get help."

"Don't worry about it, man. We'll probably be okay. Oh, I forgot to mention. I saw one of those seal thigh dinos in the furniture shop."

"Seal thigh? You are such a dork. They are pronounced Coelophysis."

"Whatever. Anyway, this guy ended up being another dinosaur's dinner. It just reached down and bit its head clean off. A real big bastard it was too. In fact, that little guy in Alan's pet shop, trying to eat all those bats with beaks, looks just like it."

"Oh fuck."

The blood had drained from David's face. He wrenched the bat out of Jefferson's hand before pressing his back tightly against the wall.

"There might have been two of them, David," said Janine.

"What are we going to do?"

"We make our way onto the next level. We look for Sandy and Alan, then find another way out of this place. Before that, I want to go back to our shop and grab a screwdriver set."

"What the hell for?"

"There's something in the sporting shop that I want."

## CHAPTER EIGHT

Zinik-Tow had already told Desmond that the shock of seeing the plague of the hairless vermin infecting and ruining the planet was enough evidence to prove that the sons of Maulis-Bow had been right all along about denying their true nature. He'd explained that the great deity didn't want any of his creations to evolve and flourish, to become a technically advanced society. At first, Desmond thought this featured fuckwit was banging on about the humans, until it dawned on him that he was going on about his own species.

It took Desmond a while to work out what it was trying to suggest. The feathered fuckwits use of long words confused the hell out of Desmond, but eventually, its reasoning did sink in. Somehow, this idiot believed the humans were a punishment from their Great Deity, to prove to that following the way of reason only led to destruction.

It obviously hadn't thought this one through. If the idiot hadn't set off that bomb in the first place, then none of this wouldn't have happened anyway. The feathered fuckwit reminded Desmond a lot of his granddad. Now that was one complete religious nutcase. He spent his life using the God excuse to explain everything from the crappy weather to losing his wallet at the bookies.

Desmond was the youngest boy from a large family. He had another five brothers and two sisters. His mum's sister hadn't exactly been known for her ability to keep her legs shut either back in her wilder and prettier days. She had given poor Desmond five older cousins, who just loved knocking the crap out of their ugly cousin. Thankfully, the beatings were few and far between as the two families only met up once a month, when they all converged on their grandparent's place for Sunday lunch.

While Gran entertained the adults, Granddad took the kids upstairs, out of the way. If it hadn't been for the others, Desmond might have enjoyed playing with the old toys and listening to his granddad bang on about the evils of the world and how God came down harshly on any bastard who stepped out of line.

He sighed heavily. Perhaps if Granddad had looked a little closer to home, he might have noticed a few bastards stepping out of line as soon as the old man left the room to visit the toilet. As soon as they were alone, his cousins took turns punching Desmond in the guts or nipping him, or slapping his face, while Desmond's brothers looked on, giggling away.

Granddad visited the toilet a lot in those days.

After Granddad died, Desmond used to wonder why the old man's God never bothered to tell granddad to get himself checked out. They might have detected the bowel cancer early enough to do something about it.

The old man's God obviously thought that telling him that it would be pissing down when he went to collect his horse race winnings was more important.

Even so, despite his grandad's dodgy interpretation of God, the old man had been the only person who'd ever treated poor Desmond with any respect when he was growing up. Perhaps his religious ideas weren't as daft as he once thought?

After all, Desmond was still here, walking around this mall, still alive and relatively safe, unlike all the other poor buggers who'd been caught up in all the excitement. Oh, Desmond didn't put his narrow escape from the jaws of death down to his granddad's God, fuck no. He put it down to meeting someone who acted just like that mental old bastard.

Zinik-Tow told Desmond that the Great Deity had allowed their species to conquer their planet before reaching for the stars. In the millions of years since discovering warp drive, they'd colonised the nearby star systems, encountering over two hundred other sentient species as they spread throughout the outer spiral arm. Naturally, their species believed that the Great Deity had placed these alien races on those planets just to taunt the species, implying they should have reached these planets long before such lesser creatures could develop to become an embarrassment to the Great Deity. Consequently, they had wiped them out.

His new pal explained that he believed his species shouldn't have used kinetic warheads on their planets followed by the release of millions of assault drop-troops landing on the surface, ready to vaporise anyone still standing once they had demolished their cities. Zinik-Tow said that using such advanced weaponry against creatures who couldn't defend themselves was blasphemy. The Great Deity created them to hunt and to kill their prey in face-to-face combat. Where was the honour to their God into turning a city of millions into molten slag from the safety of an orbiting weapons platform?

If it was truly necessary to conquer the galaxy, then instead of taking a few days to annihilate the new alien races they encountered, the species should follow The Sons of Maulis-Bow and show the proper respect to The Great Deity by hunting them down in a more appropriate manner. Why should it matter that the extermination would take a couple of years?

Back in that chamber, with the dinosaur sleeping with her head resting on her blood-stained claws, Zinik-Tow had spoken in great detail over his plans to complete to work of The Sons of Maulis-Bow. First, there would be a great purge, to remove most of the hairless vermin before starting work to create a new species, combining his advanced DNA with his ancient ancestor. The combined creation would spend their lives hunting the remaining humans and mating, as The Great Deity had intended.

Desmond had no issue with his new pal's grand plan, especially as he'd be spending all his time impregnating the females to ensure the new species had a sufficient stock of young prey to hunt and eat. The thought of him producing hundreds of annoying brats for Zinik-Tow's creations to eat pleased him greatly.

His new pal's companions couldn't be allowed to win. That's for sure, not after what Zinik-Tow had told him. He had asked the feathered fuckwit why they didn't just time travel back to the past and stop Zinik-Tow before he could set off his bomb. If they did that, then everything would be put back right. Desmond had obviously asked this question after his new pal explained that the quantum chamber, currently wedged in Martin's Department Store, stored the whole knowledge of their species advancements in its data storage crystals. His new pal patiently explained that the materials needed for the quantum chamber's repair were located on just two planets, the nearest one was thirty-four light years away. Also, the commander would have no wish to go back and fix the past. Why should he want to do that? Thanks to Zinik-Tow's bomb, he now had the opportunity to building up the species from scratch. He would see this as the ultimate gift from The Great Deity. To go back would mean the commander's name would be forgotten within a few thousand years. This way, his revered name would fall off the lips of his descendants for millions of years in the future.

Desmond had asked whether any of his pals had families and wouldn't any of them want to go back to be reunited. His new pal didn't understand the question. He then thought of his mum who ignored Desmond. His siblings and cousins who used to beat on him. Desmond then remembered his own dad telling his young son that he was a mistake, and if he had his way, he would have drowned the little fucker in the hospital toilets before they even had chance to come back home.

"Apart from three technicians who will be monitoring and perhaps attempting to repair some of the systems damaged in the explosion, the rest of the crew will be on this level of the vermin-built hive."

"It's called a shopping mall." Desmond almost called his new pal a *feathered fuckwit* but managed to bite his tongue. He was sure Zinik-Tow wouldn't understand the reference, but he'd certainly understand the implication. "So, this is your timeship?" he murmured, so wanting to run his fingers down the smooth contours of its shell. His new pal had brought him up to the second floor in the large department store. They'd walked straight past three other feathered fuckwits and four humans. It made Desmond's day when the humans, despite their predicament, shrank back as he and Zinik-Tow marched past them. His new pal had used that gizmo on Desmond, so he now looked just like a feathered fuckwit as well.

Desmond had wondered what was going to happen to the four humans and why the feathered fuckwits had made them all stand on the roof of that car. In the end, he realised that he didn't really care. One of the men was Mr. Dillon. He was the manager of the Happy Mex, a taco-themed restaurant next to the mall cinema. He once threatened this poor janitor to throw him out of the window if he ever caught Desmond rifling through the bins behind the shop.

Their timeship was nestled between the store's cafe and the cookshop. Right beside Desmond's hand was half a kettle and a quarter of a sandwich maker. Their ship had sliced a large crescent through the entire shelf. Zinik-Tow had explained to Desmond about what had happened to the rest of the stuff now occupied by their fancy time machine, but Desmond's brain went for a hike when the feathered fuckwit came out with words like *displacement physics* and *quantum compression.*

"Are you sure it's safe to go in? I mean, there won't be any cameras or some kind of laser guns embedded into the walls?"

Zinik-Tow didn't even bother to reply. He slid his claws into five recessed holes in the oval doorway. He then uttered a combination of growls and hisses. Desmond guessed that he was hearing how they spoke to each other. Unreal. To him, it sounded like sausages sizzling in a frying pan. A thick grey membrane split in two and rolled back, revealing a dark interior. His new pal then fastened his claws over Desmond's arm and dragged him inside the ship.

His new pal took his claws off Desmond once the membrane had rolled back. It took a great deal of effort to stop him from spinning around and sinking his nails into that grey stuff that looked like skin. He wanted to rip his way out of here and into proper sanitised white light instead of all this dirty-green glow, which seeped out from the numerous slits in the curved wall.

"I don't want to be in here." Desmond stopped beside a transparent panel, which moved. It looked like it was breathing. "Oh fuck, I'm in hell." He would have tried to escape if his new pal hadn't reached out and grabbed him again.

"Come. We must hurry. The power for my image resonator will not sustain the increased outage for a finite period."

Desmond groaned aloud and did as he was told. He could do that. He'd been following orders, which he hated, for most of his life. He passed more breathing panels, organic tubes, bright blue cubes made from what looked like crystal, and dozens more membrane doors. As they moved in a straight line, it dawned of Desmond that they should have run out of weird, disturbing corridors ages ago. How was that even possible? By now, they should be out of the mall and in the middle of the city centre.

He kept quiet about this, but Desmond couldn't stop himself from asking one question that his new pal had repeatedly refused to answer ever since leaving the chamber. "Are you going to tell me now what we're supposed to be doing in here?" He thought the feathered fuckwit was going to ignore him again until he stopped and turned to face Desmond.

"Desmond. It has been my observation that even for a hairless vermin, your mental facility is not that advanced. Would you not just prefer to obey my commands without me having explain myself?"

He shook his head. "Please?" Desmond jumped away from one of the blue crystal cubes when it began to oscillate.

"It is very simple. Back home, we use pacifiers to ensure the herds do not deviate from their trails. It is a perfectly acceptable method to control the lower lifeforms." Zinik-Tow performed a very passable version of a human grin. "It does not surprise me that something we use on brainless sauropods works just as well on you hairless vermin."

"Okay, so we're a lower lifeform. I get that. You still haven't told me anything." That blue cube had now returned to its previous state. "Why are we here, Zinik-Tow?"

"I am constantly surprised at how your species was able to climb down from the tree without assistance. Desmond. I turn off the field. The hairless vermin do what all herds do in this situation. They panic and stampede. Giving us the diversion in order to leave this hive."

A thin line appeared down the middle of the breathing panel behind the blue cube. The panel split and rolled back, revealing another chamber. Bright blue light spilled out and showed Desmond the first truly beautiful sight he'd seen since entering this hellish place. "Oh God! That's the hot chick from the nail bar. What's she doing in here?" He ran through the opening into the next room. Desmond moved past the two men, both fastened to long slabs with ropes of black shiny material. He stopped by Sandy and dug his fingers into the stuff tying the woman to the bed and tried to pull it away.

"Don't just stand there, help me get this off her."

"Why?"

"Because, *I want her*. That's why. You said I would be impregnating females. Well, I want to start with this one." He screamed out in rage and hurt when he broke one of his nails in the black stuff. "Come on, help me here!"

"You are in no position to make any demands. By rights, you are my slave. Slaves should only obey without asking questions, without needing to understand, and without making demands." He turned around. "Now come along, slave, or do I have to leave you here and find myself another one? As I do not think you are the only individual who wishes to live."

"Oh for crying out loud, you feathered fuckwit. Just seeing it as doing me a favour. As for finding another one like me, good luck with that. See, most of these people around here have something which I don't possess, they're called principles, integrity, and empathy. They'll see you and want to murder you. It's that's simple. They'll do everything in their power to make sure you and your kind are exterminated."

Zinik-Tow approached Desmond, and for the first time, he saw the size of those talons on the creature's hands. It didn't take much imagination to see how much damage they could do to Desmond's soft flesh if this feathered fuckwit decided he wasn't needed anymore. He wrapped his fingers tighter around the stuff holding her to the slab and tried not to shiver in fright as the creature leaned over his shoulder.

"Tell me again why you want me to unshackle this particular female."

He jerked his head away from the creature's hot breath, totally thrown by this turn of events. Was he playing with Desmond? He was painfully aware of just how close those talons were to his balls. Was Zinik-Tow going to castrate him as soon as he repeated his intentions as a punishment? Oh God, this situation was almost unbearable. He was so close to hanging his head in shame and apologising when the tips of his fingers found Sandy's soft, warm skin and the thought of making love to this beautiful woman from now until the end of time drown out every other thought. It even stamped on Desmond's well-tuned instinct for self-preservation.

"I want this woman to be my mate, Zinik-Tow. I want to do things to her that would make a porn star blush. I want to—"

"Enough. You have said enough." The creature pushed a claw into a hole in the slab underneath Sandy's head. "I believe that we both have understood your intentions."

He watched the black cord-like material untangle and retreat into the edge of the grey slab. The girl's eyes flickered. Desmond sighed inwardly. He had never seen a more sightly woman. He felt like a prince awakening sleeping beauty. There were going to live happy ever after as well. Desmond wanted to turn around and thank Zinik-Tow for making his dream come true, but he dare not take his eyes from her. He couldn't wait for her to thank him for saving her life.

Sandy snapped open her eyes. She must have seen the creature standing behind Desmond and assumed he was one of her captors. She let out a quiet sob before cringing back from Desmond's hand.

"Keep away from me, you vile thing!"

Desmond blinked, momentarily confused. Was she talking to him?

"You fucking dirty old bastard!" she snapped. The woman jumped off the other side of the slab and ran into the corner of the room. "I wouldn't be your mate if my life depended on it."

"You don't understand, you stupid bitch!" he shouted. "Your life does depend on it." Desmond turned and glared at Zinik-Tow. "Why didn't you tell me? I thought she was going to be like all those bubble-headed idiots out there!"

"The field in nullified in here. I thought that would be obvious." The creature then wrapped those claws around Desmond's throat. "You are but a herd animal. You are livestock, nothing more. Do not forget your place again or the consequences will be unfortunate." He picked him up and carried Desmond out of the room. He dropped him on the floor and sealed the door. "You can find your way to the chamber on your own, Desmond. If you are lucky, it is quite possible you will get there without anything eating you. Farewell." He turned around and stormed down the corridor and disappeared through another membrane.

Desmond to his feet and raced after him, only to discover the membrane wouldn't fold back. "Wait, come back! Don't leave me in here. I don't know the way back." His calls went unanswered. Desmond walked back to that blue cube, now noticing that he could see into the other room. The girl saw him staring and gave Desmond the finger before she buried her head back in her arms.

"Yeah well, fuck you too," he snarled before shuffling off in what he hoped was the right way to get out of this hellish place.

## CHAPTER NINE

That old woman wearing an oversized brown coat had just spat at him. Her reaction took Steven White totally by surprise. He picked up the *animal cruelty* booklet which she had dropped in the gutter and folded it in half, idly wiping off some of the wet black slime that had just leaked out one of the seeping blisters on his index finger.

Maybe he should get over to the train station. It'll be rush hour soon. There'll be plenty of customers disembarking from the packed trains. Some of them are bound to take his remaining booklets. He really did want to go home and crawl into bed. Since meeting up with that very nice Mr. Smith inside the mall, he hadn't been feeling that great. Steven had noticed how moist he was getting under these clothes as well. As if his skin was slipping around his muscles. It sure was a weird feeling.

Still, he had a promise to keep and that's exactly what he was going to do. Steven White never backed out on a promise, that's for sure. Besides, it wouldn't take him that long to hand out the last of his booklets. Just another few more minutes, and he'd be able to go home and have a soak in a nice warm bath before crawling into bed.

Steven bent over to scratch a particularly itchy spot under his socks, a little confused to find two more of his fingernails must have dropped off. No matter, he rolled up the booklet, pulled the sock down, and used the edge of the card instead.

He sighed loudly as the card scraped the jelly-like flesh away from his bone. Steven didn't realise that his body was slowly dissolving, nor did he care. All that mattered was to deliver every single booklet and to touch as many people as possible. It's what Mr. Smith had ordered him to do.

His girl, Lisa, would have a right fit if she saw the state of his socks. He had no idea how he'd managed to get all this weird goo all over them, but he knew she wouldn't be happy if she saw them. Maybe Steven could take them off before he got home and drop them in the bin outside. She'd be none the wiser. He certainly did feel funny.

It took him a few seconds to realise what he was supposed to be doing. It wasn't until he heard one of the trains pulling into the station, on the other side of the square, when he remembered. Steven grinned, spitting out three of his front teeth. That's right, it was the rush hour. There were soon going to be hundreds of people about to brush past him.

It wasn't just the prospect of all those people which gave him cause for happiness, oh no. He had made over three hundred pounds today as well. Gavin at the Animal Care Foundation was going to be *over the moon* with the amount of cash he was going to hand over. Oh, Gavin wasn't going to get all of it, no chance. Steven intended to put away a hundred so he could buy himself a decent phone. Why not? It's about time he bought something for himself for a change. Gavin wouldn't mind, basically because he wasn't going to tell him.

Who said being nosy didn't pay dividends? Oh, that's right, his girl said those exact words to him only this morning. That's cool. It just meant she wouldn't have half of the pizza he would be ordering once Steven climbed out of the bath. He took a couple of steps forward and stopped beside a low wall. It was no good, he would have to take a breather. He sat on the wall and looked back the way he came, watching a man over the road on his knees. It looked like he was coughing up blood. Simon was sure that he gave a booklet to that guy a few minutes ago.

Thanks to Steven's nosiness, the phone that he'd clocked this morning would be in his pocket this time tomorrow. Moe's Mobile Shop had a huge selection in their window. He passed the place every day, and it made him so annoyed to think that he'd never have enough money to afford one. He should also thank that rude boy too, the one who worked in that discount shop. After all, it's him who got Steven inside, even if he wasn't aware of it.

He had already been around the back of the mall a few minutes after the shutters came down unexpectedly, and it did come as a bit of a surprise to find another set of shutters over the entrance to the furniture shop. He was sure they weren't there the last time he was around here. That was a couple of weeks, though, so he just guessed he'd been blind.

Steven got the shock of his life when the rude boy just seemingly passed straight through the metal. He wasn't shocked enough to leave it alone, no chance of that. He crossed the distance between the corner of the mall and those pretend shutters in less than a minute. He waited for two girls to pass him before he investigated these mysterious shutters.

He could see the rude boy on the other side of them making his way further into the interior of the shop. Steven couldn't see anybody else in there. He counted to five before closing his eyes and walking forward, expecting his nose to smash into the metal. Apart from a fleeting feeling of finding himself wanting to go back to work and the need to make friends, Steven's nose surprisingly stayed intact.

His recollection became a little hazy once he had wandered into the furniture shop. Steven did recall seeing a couple of people, dressed up as dinosaurs, running from one shop into another. It was just a shame that there were no shoppers about to see the costumes; the detailing was fantastic. He guessed they must have either been in the eatery or in the restaurants on the next level. He shook his head, trying to clear his thoughts. Had he blacked out or something? He did remember having to sit on the side of a bed. There was a guy in front of him, only it wasn't a guy. Maybe it was another one of those festival people, only this one was dressed like some big yellow bird. Did this bird do something to him? Steven frowned, remembering some fragment of this bird pushing a needle into his left arm. No, that couldn't have happened. The whole idea was just too ridiculous for words. He must have dozed off for a second. That bed was very comfy.

That nice Mr. Smith got Steven back on his feet again. Such a pleasant chap. His dress style was a little outlandish, though. He wasn't sure why Smith thought looking like some nineteenth century gentleman, complete with top hat and cane, was a proper way to dress. Then again, who was he to criticise, considering his dreadlocks came halfway down the tattered US army coat that never came off his back? His girl had even threatened to burn the bloody thing on more than one occasion. Still, it was a little weird how the nice Mr. Smith looked exactly like the poster on the wall, coming down the stairs from the upper level.

Obviously, Smith had come from the horse races. It would explain the outfit and why he handed over so much money to a complete stranger.

As for the insistence of Steven to hand out every one of his booklets while making sure he touched every person, well, *the guy was on a guilt trip*, it stood to reason.

Steven eased himself off the wall, shedding some more of his liquefying flesh. There were a few more people across the square on their knees now. He shrugged to himself. There must be something going around. He wasn't exactly feeling that great himself. The tip of his index finger snapped off when Steven scratched the top of his head.

He watched as the train stopped and the automatic doors opened. Like an overstuffed cushion, the contents spilled out onto the platform. Steven shuffled towards the ticket barrier, eager to touch as many of commuters as he could.

## CHAPTER TEN

The doors leading to the next level came into sight just as the eruption of human screams blasted out from the floor above. It wasn't just from above them. Jefferson jumped back, almost tumbling back down the steps, when a shriek erupted from Janine as well.

The woman let go of his hand. She slammed her palm over her mouth and pressed her body against the wall in the stairwell, looking at the two boys, in utter horror.

Jefferson listened to the screams from beyond the doors die down until all he could hear was moans and groaning.

"Honey, are you okay?" he asked.

She nodded. "Thanks, I'm fine, thank you. Please though, don't call me that. I'm old enough to be your mother."

David giggled. "Looks like your sci-fi gas has worn off. I should have known."

Jefferson resisted the impulse put a crossbow bolt through the side of David's head. He also resisted the urge to cry. God, he really was beginning to grow fond of this woman as well. "Can you tell me what you last remember?" He fully expected her to tell him and David that she knew nothing after opening up, that the effect of whatever their intruders had injected into the mall had made her forget everything.

She glanced up at the double doors before turning her attention back to him. "Jefferson, I remember everything, and it makes me feel…" She shook her head. "Look, forget it. I think we have more important issues to resolve."

The woman looked at the katana she held in her hand, as if it was the first time she had seen it, despite helping David unscrew them from the wall of the sporting shop.

David held the other katana while Jefferson held his prized crossbow.

He couldn't argue with her, no matter how much Jefferson so wanted to, not when there was too much at stake. They still need to find his other friends, and Jefferson had no idea what faced them on this level. He guessed that there'd be more dinosaurs up here and believed they'd have to face whoever or whatever had done this to the mall. Jefferson notched a bolt and ran up the remaining steps with the two others bringing up the rear.

"Are you ready?" he asked. Jefferson didn't wait for a reply before he silently pushed open the door. He saw a couple of shoppers running out of the Happy Mex restaurant and down the wide corridor which led to the restrooms. He saw nobody else. Still, finding somebody up here alive and kicking gave him hope.

Jefferson slithered through the door, holding it open for the other two. "I've just seen a couple of people running out of the restaurant!" It was about time they had some good news. Jefferson was about to follow the shoppers when both David and Janine cried out. They both stared past Jefferson, their eyes bulging. He spun around and gasped out when the reason for *fleeing shoppers* became apparent.

Ducking its huge head so it could squeeze the rest of its huge body through the doorway, a monster which almost made Jefferson lose control of his bladder, moved that jaw bristling with curved teeth. The teeth were the size of Jefferson's little finger. He felt a pair of hands trying to pull him back into the stairwell, but he shrugged them off. He wasn't going to run, not now.

The large dinosaur dropped its head to the floor and sniffed at the tiles. It was acting as though he wasn't even there! Jefferson then noticed the few spots of blood. He raised the crossbow, making he sure made no sudden moves.

The dinosaur then jerked up its head, switching its gaze from the corridor. The dinosaur's eyes finally settled on Jefferson. It growled before running straight at him.

He squeezed the trigger before he dropped to the floor and rolled out of the way. The sudden roar of pain, which almost burst his eardrums, told Jefferson that his bolt had hit home, but the bastard still lived. The creature's large shadow turned his world dark. He rolled again, just avoiding the wounded dinosaur's sharp teeth as it lunged forward, its jaws snapping shut exactly where Jefferson's head used to be. The crossbow flew from his grip and skittered along the floor. He managed to get to his feet and reach the edge of the next restaurant. His fingers curled around the back of a metal chair.

He spun around, ready for this roaring behemoth to lunge at him again, only to discover the creature dancing with both Janine and David while they slashed at its flesh with their swords. He let go of the chair, scooped up his crossbow, and managed to push his foot through the stirrup and pull back the string without slipping. He heard the sounds of crying and whimpering. It took Jefferson a moment to realise the noises were coming from him.

He notched in a bolt and ran towards his friends, needing to put this monster down before the creature killed them both.

Janine brought the sword down on the base of its tail, the blade sank deep into the flesh.

Jefferson watched in horror when the dinosaur twisted like a ballet dancer. She lost her grip on the weapon and its tail whipped around, sweeping David off his feet.

It lunged at the woman, those wicked fangs missing the top of her head by inches. Luckily, the woman saw that massive head falling towards her and dropped to the floor. It raised its foot.

Jefferson's heart missed a beat. It was going to pin her to the floor!

"Over here, you *scaly bastard*!" he yelled, running up to it. Jefferson's shout went unheeded; the thing must have decided that he wasn't worth bothering with. He went down on one knee, steadied his aim, and fired. The bolt plunged into the dinosaur's huge eye.

"And fuck you too!" he shouted when it fell forwards and slammed onto the floor. Jefferson jumped over its tail and ran over to Janine. "Oh God, I thought I had lost you!" He helped her up, deliriously happy to be holding her hand again, even if it was for a few seconds.

Jefferson retrieved her katana and helped David up. He brushed himself down and grinned at the pair of them.

"What a rush!"

"I'll agree to that, David," she said. "Who needs a gym membership when you can fight dinosaurs?"

These two wouldn't even be alive if it hadn't been for his quick reactions. Jefferson kept that little info nugget to himself. "We'd better go see if those people are okay." He loaded his crossbow, hoping he'd have enough bolts to last. If they encountered any more of these buggers though, Jefferson decided that their lifespan would be measured in minutes. "Come on, guys, we had better get a move…" His remaining words dried up when he saw they were no longer alone.

"No," hissed David, when Jefferson raised his crossbow. "That pack of *Coelophysis* aren't here for us."

Several of the little brown dinosaurs were dancing and hopping across the concourse, their heads darting left and right. Two of them jumped onto a table a few feet from where they stood, each one issuing bird-like chirps.

David quickly wiped his sword clean on the fallen dinosaur and motioned Janine to do the same. He then grabbed Jefferson's arm. "We need to get past them."

"Are you having a laugh?" Two on the table had now jumped off and were heading straight for them, he could hear their jaws snapping shut.

"Are *you* having a laugh, dude?" The two small dinosaurs on the table leaped off and were now heading straight for them. He heard their jaws snapping shut. "We should get those others out of toilets before it's too late!"

Jefferson felt so betrayed when Janine skirted past him and joined David as he slowly edged along the wall. The two dinosaurs now became four, then five, as more of them skittered closer to the corpse.

"Leave them, Jefferson!" David commanded. "Seriously. It's already is too late. They'll be fine as long as they don't leave."

"But one bite!"

Janine ran over to him and grabbed his hand. "Do as you're bleeding told!" The woman pulled him over to David. She didn't even give the two little dinosaurs that ran past them a single glance. She gently squeezed his hand, her grip becoming tighter when the rest of the excitable animals raced over to the corpse. He heard them fighting amongst themselves, each one trying their hardest to stay on top of the dead dinosaur's head. He looked away when one of them pushed its snout into the corpse's damaged eye.

"That's a *Troodon*!" gasped, David. "I've never seen one so big before. I bet nobody has."

"See a lot of them, do you?" snapped Jefferson. "Oh yeah. Shit, I forgot about the dinosaur family who pop into our shop every Saturday. They love the doggy treats. Don't blame them, you won't find them cheaper anywhere else."

"Are you done?"

He turned on David. "No, I'm not fucking done. Look at your seal thigh thingies. Just look at them, for crying out loud. How are we going to help those people trapped in there now? Oh God, listen to me. I'm a dinosaur expert. I know all their names and everything. Everybody follow me. When, in fact, you know shit!" Jefferson rested his back against the glass front of a sushi restaurant, panting like a knackered dog. He knew he'd just gone too far, that him lashing out at his friend was purely from fear as well as frustration. He couldn't find a way to stop his mouth from running off.

Jefferson turned around, he knew he should apologise, but he just couldn't do it. He didn't want to look at their faces anymore. He saw half a dozen people in the restaurant. Every one of them were staring right back at him. Jefferson felt like sticking out his tongue.

"Listen to the man of action. The hero of the flipping day. Listen, Jefferson. If you hadn't been showing off in front of your girlfriend, that *Troodon* wouldn't have even noticed us. No, not you. You just had to shoot at it and piss it off."

Jefferson tried not to jump when David spun him around.

"As for not knowing shit."

He thrust his fingers under Jefferson's jaw and savagely twisted his head to the side. Another two smaller species were hovering around the perimeter. They and the Coelophysis all scattered when two larger animals appeared on the scene. Jefferson realised that the new arrivals looked exactly like the one he had brought down, just a little smaller.

"A large kill always attracts attention. It's what's happening now, so it stands to reason that it's what would have happened back when these monsters ruled the planet as opposed to a shopping mall. Now, just imagine us running out of those bogs with our rescued people. How many of those things will the *mighty hero* take down before we all get ripped apart?"

Jefferson peeled David's fingers away. He looked at the boy and sighed. "Sorry, man. I was out of order." He pulled David into an embrace. "I'm an idiot." Over his shoulder, he saw Janine talking to one of the people who'd ventured out of the restaurant. Judging from the changing expression on Janine's face, the people up here hadn't exactly had an easy time of it either.

He wanted to shout out to Janine and get her to find out if any of them knew what was going on. Jefferson decided to keep his gob shut, at least until he reached the strangers. He was sure that Janine will have already asked this question. Blurting out the same thing with all those meat-eating dinosaurs within sight wouldn't be one of his better ideas. He released David and watched his mate silently wander over to the others, leaving Jefferson alone.

Had he really been showing off to impress Janine? No, that wasn't true. He only wanted to protect them, wanted to make sure his friends were safe. Christ, surely David didn't really think that? He watched his friend slip into his standard behaviour pattern, now that he had a captive audience, no doubt telling all how these fuckers romped about in their natural habitat. Basically doing exactly what David accused him of doing. The annoying turd was showing off. By the looks of the way events were progressing, Jefferson would soon have to rescue the idiot as well.

It didn't surprise Jefferson to note that one particular individual had taken an instant dislike to David. As per usual, David was completely oblivious to the danger.

He walked over to the three people who'd left the restaurant to greet Janine and David. Jefferson didn't recognise the big man and the smaller blonde woman standing by his side. Although he guessed they were attached, judging for the way the woman's dark green eyes kept darting from the man beside her, to David, and back again. There was also the weird way she kept tugging at the man's green trousers. She reminded Jefferson of an eager dog trying to get her master's attention.

He had seen the other woman talking to Janine. She worked in the scented candle shop next to the pet shop, on the far side of this level. Both Alan and Sandy spent a fortune in there every week.

Jefferson never saw the attraction of forking out a bloody fortune for a few candles that smelled of flowers or sickly fruit. Not when a can of air freshener would do the job just as effectively.

He remembered all those times in that shop, bored out of his pissing mind, watching those two push candles against their noses. Right now, he would do anything to travel back in time to one of those occasions. Oh God, just listen to him banging on about time travel. He was getting as bad as David.

Speaking of David, if he didn't do anything soon, that big man, who his friend was unwittingly pissing off, looked like he was about to crack the lad with that broken table leg he held in that troll-sized hand. It didn't escape Jefferson's attention that the splintered end was stained with wet blood. It did please him to find that it wasn't just their little gang who was fighting back. He just hoped that the blood belonged to a dinosaur, and not another clever dick who also had an encyclopaedic knowledge of sodding dinosaur names.

"No, you're wrong, glasses boy. We were all doing just fine until you and Rambo here bumbled up here with your noise and fancy crossbow."

It took Jefferson a moment for him to realise that the shaved gorilla was talking about him. He would have said something back if this fool wasn't holding that table leg. Then again, maybe not. This guy would look formidable holding an egg whisk.

"You take no notice of our Kevin," said the woman, squeezing past the man's bulky gut. "We've not had the best of days, you see." She leaned to one side, staring at the noisy animals ripping into that carcass. "Those things aren't helping either. People ought to be ashamed of themselves, letting their dogs off the lead all the time."

Jefferson's eyes flickered across to David's twitching face, praying that the lad wasn't going to burst out in a fit of giggles.

"What have I told you, Margaret? I'm dealing with it." He pushed her behind him. "Why don't you go back inside and see if your new friends want another cup of tea?"

"Well, if you say so, Kevin. You just be nice to these kiddies and don't take too long. Remember, we're supposed to be visiting

Uncle George this evening, and you know jittery he gets when we're late."

"Yes, dear," he replied, pushing the woman closer to the open doorway. Why couldn't they have found a squad of off-duty soldiers or even a few police marksmen who'd gotten themselves caught up in here? Trust him to bump into a pair of outcasts from the Addams's Family.

The middle-aged woman, wearing a very fetching lime-green knitted cardigan and a shit-brown pleated skirt, gave Jefferson a little wave and a big smile before she disappeared inside. He turned to find the other half of this mad pair glowering at him and his crossbow.

He would have preferred this ape to have gone inside instead of her. She might have been as *mad as a box of frog*, but at least she didn't look like she wanted to pull off Jefferson's head. He wondered if Janine would be upset if he accidentally shot him in the face.

"Why don't you and your lot just bugger off back to your own level? We were doing just fine until you lot blundered up here with your noise."

"Noise? What noise, big fella?" asked David. "We have a crossbow and swords, not grenades."

The other woman left Janine and rested her hand on the man's wrist. "Easy now, Kevin." She gently stroked his lower arm. "Do you know what I've left inside? I've only come out here and left my glasses on my table. Could you be a dear and get them for me?"

"Wait, what about these guys? I mean, they've made so much noise and I've told them to bugger off and everything. They're going to bring the others down here. The nasty ones with guns and everything. I really don't like those."

"Don't you worry about it, Kevin," she said. "I'll sort it. While you're in there, go have another ice cream." She winked. "I promise I won't tell Margaret."

Jefferson could listen to her silky tones all day. This was so weird. He never knew the woman had such a sensuous voice. Granted, most of the times he heard her speak, she was asking for money while standing behind her till. Her words did have the desired effect, though. The big guy nodded once before following the mad woman inside.

The remaining woman waited until he was out of sight before turning around and resting her back against the wall. "Bloody hell, that fella is hard work." She stuck out her hand, which Jefferson dutifully shook. "Still, without him and his table leg, we'd have all been dino food ages ago. He sure can fight."

"I'm Jefferson," he said, lamely.

The woman laughed. "You're cute. I can see why Janine's taken a shine to you."

"Stop it, Lindsey!"

"Stop what? I'm only making an observation, honey. You know me." She smiled at Jefferson. "Even under these dire circumstances, it's nice to find someone who's melted the heart of the ice-maiden. As you've heard, I'm Lindsey." She looked past Jefferson and David. "Kevin did have a point about the noise, though. Come on, you'd better come inside. I don't think it would take much longer for those horrible things to finish off their meal."

Jefferson slyly punched David in the back to ensure the goon wouldn't spoil everything by opening his mouth to give out another pointless fact about dinosaur feeding times. He could still taste Janine's lipstick from the last time they'd kissed.

She directed them to a table by the window. "I know you're brimming with questions, and you're desperate to find your friends." She held up her hand when Jefferson opened his mouth. "Don't worry, cutie. Janine's already filled me in on the valid points." She sat down opposite Jefferson. "She told me that you two weren't affected."

"What do you mean?" Jefferson asked.

"She means your sci-fi gas, you idiot." David grinned. "That's what you mean, it is, isn't it?"

Jefferson tried not to smile when this new woman gave David that look, the one Sandy always saved especially for his annoying friend. "No, I came in from outside. He was doing what he always does when our boss leaves the shop, he skived in the toilets." He looked out of the window and saw the bigger dinosaurs had left the carcass to the smaller ones now. How many of the mall's shoppers had fallen to those bastards? It must have been absolute pandemonium up here, if this was where everybody had come to. His mind showed him hundreds of panicking people running in all directions while those things leaped on their backs, or knocked them down, before ripping into their soft bodies.

He took his eyes off the mixed collection of little dinosaurs fighting over what was left of that body and scanned what he could see of the concourse floor. There were a few bloodied footprints on the tiles, but they belonged to the dinosaurs. Even if they had eaten everything including the bones, there should still have been some evidence left behind. He doubted they would have eaten the shoes, mobile phones, pushchairs, and backpacks.

The thought of that miserable janitor wheeling his squeaky trolley down the concourse sprang to mind, picking up bits of chewed-up meat, ripped clothing, and dumping them in his trolley before he mopped up all the blood. It was such a ridiculous idea, and yet, he could still picture that weirdo doing just that. His name was *Desmond*; he was sure of it.

Jefferson jumped when Janine sat down beside him, and her fingers slipped into his.

"We were like obedient little sheep," muttered Lindsey. "I must have been one of the first ones to succumb to it. One minute, I was serving that couple over there, Kevin and Margaret, the next, I was walking straight out of my shop with those two behind me. There must have been well over a hundred people standing in between the shops, all still and every one of them with a strange smile plastered across their face. I guess I must have looked the same as them too. What I found more frightening than anything was the silence. All I heard was the jolly tunes playing over the tannoy system. I was screaming, Jefferson. Shrieking until I was blue in the face, and yet just like the others in that crowd, I never made a sound." She sighed heavily. "I'm sorry. I don't want to continue. The memories are too bitter." She looked over to the mad couple. "Those two weren't so off-kilter when they first came into my shop. This *whatever it was* has screwed up their minds. I guess that if we do get out of here in one piece, that couple will be in therapy for a long time."

Janine squeezed his hand. "That's a little what I felt like, I guess. Only a lot milder." She gazed at Jefferson. "You could say I was under the influence when my knight saved me from the dragon."

David made vomiting sounds.

Lindsey leaned over the table and tapped on the glass. "The ones who did this to us are all congregated close to Martin's." She looked at Jefferson. "That's where the rest of them are. I guess it's where you'll find your friends as well."

"Who are they?" asked David. "Come on, don't keep us in the dark. What do they want with us?" He turned to Jefferson. "A tenner says they're aliens."

"Will you shut your gob for a second?" He guessed that they were directly above Sandy's Beauty Parlour, and as the level followed the plan of the ground floor, they would need to get past the shopping centre's cinema to see the other end of the mall. He saw no movement outside now, even the little dinosaurs had moved away. Still, it didn't mean that there wouldn't be anything waiting for them as soon as they left the relative safety of this restaurant. "I'm sorry about him, Lindsey, he's a constant embarrassment. Are you staying here?"

She shook her head. "No, we only stopped here because we saw that big dead thing's head poking out of the Happy Mex. That's when your lot showed up. We're going to try and get onto the roof." She pulled out her mobile phone. "Once we're outside, I'm hoping that my life support machine will start working again. To be honest, I can't think of any other way out of here. We've already tried a couple of fire doors, and Janine has already told me about what it's like downstairs."

"There's still the furniture shop exit I told you about, remember," said Janine. "I bet we'll be able to get out that way."

Jefferson heard the words but didn't want to believe them. She said *we*. Janine was going with them, leaving him to find Sandy and Alan alone. He bet David would leave him as well.

Janine reached down and pulled out her sword. She carefully placed it on the table. "Maybe you should let your big friend play with this. It'll be more effective than his table leg. I'm not cut out to be a ninja warrior." She rested her other hand over the back of Lindsey's other hand. "Go towards the furniture shop. I don't think you'll get out the roof way. Whoever did this will have thought of that already. Besides, it's going to be locked and bolted. We'll join you outside."

Lindsey stood. "Just be careful, all of you."

"Wait on!" said David. "You still haven't told us who's done this. Come on, lady. I have money riding on this!"

The woman calmly picked up the sword. She gestured the others over and explained the change of plans. Kevin's didn't seem that happy about this new development, but he soon changed his expression when Lindsey handed him the sword. She waited for the other five people in the restaurant to leave before she finally turned around. The woman walked straight up to David and pinned the boy against the wall. "There is a good person inside of you, David. I know there is, but it is hidden underneath all those layers of antagonistic bullshit that you use to protect and comfort your inner core. I should take your whiny arse with me and get Kevin to keep an eye on you, but I suspect he'll end up cutting off your head."

Jefferson tried to intervene, only for Janine to pull him back.

"There's a good chance that you will be responsible for the death of your friends, as well as yourself, purely because of how you act. I know there isn't a chance in hell of you coming to terms with what's happened in the shopping mall, because those protective layers won't allow it. The only reason why I'm letting you go with them is because I firmly believe you are a lucky person. It's the only reason why *Lady Karma* made you hide away. I think there's only you left in here who hasn't gone through that living nightmare of being aware but having no control over their body. It will give you an edge. You're the back-up plan if Jefferson doesn't make it."

She turned around a looked straight at Janine. "The ones who did this to us are terrible creatures. I have never seen anything like the before, but my own psyche tells me that they're not from another world or demons from the realm beyond this one. They are evil incarnate, though, and do not place any value upon our lives, except perhaps for the amusement they receive from our suffering." She sighed. "I'm sorry, Janine. My mind and my spirit is still in a great deal of pain from what they did to us. I'm just thankful that the controlling force suddenly vanished. Right now, I know I need to get these people out of here. It's my calling. Now listen to me, Janine. You alone will be helpless against them. The effect might be lifted but its vile taint still lingers. You need to remember that."

Lindsey stepped away from the boy, turned, and hugged Janine tightly. "Take care, you." She smiled at Jefferson. "That goes for you as well. Bring them all back down here, Jefferson. You are a good man, one who's true to his friends." She then winked at Janine. "If my friend hadn't already snagged your heart, I might have been tempted to try and seduce you myself."

"Just go, Lindsey," said Janine.

"Neither of you have to come with me," said Jefferson once the woman had left the restaurant. "I will understand, you know." He looked over at Janine. "You heard what she said, you won't be able to hurt the bastards who did this to us."

Janine wrapped her arms around his waist. "We won't know until we try, will we? Anyway, I'm not leaving you. I thought we'd already established that?"

"As much as I'd love to keep the company of the cave troll, I think that I'm going to take my chances with you. Besides, you heard what *Mystic Mary* said, Jeffdude." David grinned while he slapped a laminated menu on the table and tried to cut it in half with his sword. "I'm your lucky charm. Anyway, if I don't find out who's responsible for all of this mess, I'm going to go bleeding mental."

# CHAPTER ELEVEN

Somewhere behind the warm wall, the constant thudding of hidden machinery kept her focused on the task at hand. It also reminded her, that despite everything that she's endured since this nightmare began, she still lived. No matter what, Sandy intended to stay that way as well.

She moaned in disgust, as the two fingers she'd pushed into one of the numerous holes in the wall encountered what felt like thick cold jelly. No matter the impulse, she kept them in the hole, feeling through the jelly stuff, trying to find some kind of lever or button that would make the plastic curtains pull apart. She saw the dirty-minded janitor do it on that other door outside her room. So, there was no reason why she couldn't get it to work in here for her too.

Had that dirty freak managed to find a way out of here? If he had, then Sandy sure hoped that one of the lizardmen who'd completely fucked up her day had found him and slaughtered the bastard. She groaned again when the tips of her fingers found what felt like a match head. She placed her index finger on top of it, said a short prayer, and pushed down. She resisted the urge to leap up and dance when the grey curtains folded back.

She pulled her fingers out of the hole and ran through the opening before it could close. She'd done it! Sandy had got herself out of there. She wiped the gunk off her fingers and turned around, trying to figure out where to go now. There were three more curtains, each one heading off in different directions. She thought the janitor had gone through the one the lizardmen had brought her through, but she wasn't totally sure. Back then, Sandy was too busy trying to get her limbs to listen to her commands to pay too much attention to the interior of this hellish place.

It had to be that door. That janitor was bound to know the route back; after all, he'd only been inside her room for a matter of minutes. He couldn't have forgotten the way back in that time. She crouched beside the doorframe and ran her fingers down the surface, until one area felt softer than the rest. "What's wrong with a door handle?" she growled, pushing her two fingers deep inside the jelly-filled cavity. This time, it only took her a couple of seconds for her fingers to locate the device that slid the curtains apart. Sandy pushed down then stood while they opened. Beyond was yet another corridor, which looked exactly like the one she was leaving. The one difference was it only had two ways out.

Sandy jumped through the opening just before the curtains slid back. She tilted her head and gazed around where she'd found herself, vaguely wondering why such a technologically advanced race of beings didn't bother with any signs written in English and pointing to the way out. This place seriously gave her the creeps. Everything looked like it was made out of melted plastic.

If this corridor did reflect the one that she had just left, then the curtain directly in front of her must take Sandy a little closer to the final exit. It also meant that the curtain to her side might lead into a room very similar to the one she escaped from. It was so tempting to try and get out of this vile place as soon as possible, but Sandy knew that she wasn't the only captive that the lizardmen brought on board. She couldn't leave without at least making sure.

Sandy headed over to the curtain by her side. Now that she was used to how these things worked, she saw exactly where to push in her fingers, but she paused. Sandy knew the lizardmen didn't just store humans in here. While those bastards operated her like a radio-controlled toy, she saw more of the dinosaur things that had rampaged through the mall. Only these dinos were bigger, a lot bigger. What if she opened one of those by mistake? "Then I won't live long enough to care," she said. Sandy placed both her hands flat against the wall. When she passed through here the first time, there were windows along here. From the corner of her eyes, Sandy saw the big dinos pacing their cages; at least, she saw their terrible claws and their vast red and blue-skinned scales.

She dragged her fingers down the edges of the walls, feeling for any kind of depression, while wondering why all the movie dinosaurs were always a crappy brown colour, very similar to these walls. "David would have known." God, she so hoped her mates were all right. Even David. Oh sure, the lad was a total pain in the neck. He had this really annoying habit of trying to look down her top, but he wasn't a bad lad, just a bit weird. Come to think of it, David wouldn't have a clue as to why these dinosaurs were all cartoon coloured either, although he'd pretend he did know. David was good at pretending he knew everything. Hell, the goon would even pretend to know how to get this sodding window open.

After threatening to headbutt the wall, as well as calling it every swear word she could think of, her left forefinger slipped into that familiar but totally disgusting jelly substance. Banishing the thought that the jelly might be toxic to humans, Sandy fiddled about in the cavity until her finger located the catch. She silently counted to three before pushing it in. The brown wall faded away to show Sandy a room exactly like the one she'd escaped from. There were no ugly-looking dinosaurs in this one, just another slab containing a sleeping human. "Oh, thank the Lord!" she gasped when the man inside the room managed to raise his head just enough for her to recognise Alan.

She ran over to the doorway and screamed in frustration when she couldn't find the depression. "Don't worry, Alan. I'll get you out of there!" Sandy's heart then went into meltdown when her ears detected the sounds of another door close by opening. "Shit, don't need this right now." Her fingers finally found the depression. Within seconds, Sandy had the curtains open and was inside the room. She dropped and hid under the window. "Alan, put your head back down!" she hissed.

She heard the distinctive sound of the curtains folding back followed by the lizardmen's weird chatter. Two shadows fell across Alan's slab. She clenched her fingers into fists, wondering if she was strong enough to knock them out if they came into this room. They weren't exactly built like dockers. She reckoned one hard right hook would drop at least one of them before the other lizardman overpowered her. Sandy would rather die than to let those horrid bastards confine her again.

"They've gone," whispered Alan. He raised his head. "Please, get me the heck out of this thing, Sandy!"

She nodded and scuttled over to her friend. She didn't see how that other lizardman freed her, but she imagined that the process would be similar to the door mechanisms. Sandy ran her fingers along the edge while trying to calm Alan down. The poor lad was in a right state. She found what had to be the release mechanism and pushed her finger in. Just as Sandy found what felt like one of those match heads, an ear-piercing *screech* blasted through the room. The gel started to solidify. Sandy panicked and tried to pull her finger out of the thickening substance.

The doorway outside opened again, and she saw two lizardmen peering through the window, staring right at her as she attempted to remove her finger.

"Oh God, we're dead, Sandy. You shouldn't have come back for me!"

"Shush your mouth, you daft sod," she murmured, still trying to extract the tip of her finger from the now solid gel. The curtain behind her started to slide apart. Sandy dropped to the floor, she placed both her feet against the edge of the slab and pushed with all her might, ignoring the sudden pain as the solid gel refused to relinquish its hold on her skin. She was fully aware of the two lizardmen rushing towards her but didn't stop her efforts to free herself. The pain became unbearable, and she became aware of something inside her finger slip but was almost free. Sandy shrieked out and jerked her hand back, crying out in agony at the sight of her fingernail still attached to the gel.

She rolled out of the way of the lizardmen, got back on her feet, and booted the nearest one in the back of its spindly feathery leg. Sandy couldn't believe it when her former captor cried out and fell to the floor. From the angle of its legs, it was quite clear that she'd just broken its leg. Sandy grabbed the wounded lizardman's thin arm and pulled it over to the edge of the wall. She placed her foot on its broken leg and applied enough pressure to make the thing scream out even louder. "All right, you bastard. I'll make this easy for you." She pointed to the other lizardman, and then nodded over to Alan. "If you free my friend, I won't inflict any more damage on your feathered pal. Do we have a deal?" She applied a little more pressure on its broken leg to make sure her message had gone through loud and clear. Over the creature's squealing, she watched the other one rush over to the slab. Sandy bit her lip and leaned her back against the wall as the wave of pain coming from her fingertip threatened to overwhelm her. She couldn't allow that to happen. If she did fall, she doubted these two would be that merciful with her or Alan. "Come on, you shithead, do as your told!"

It chirped out some more of its nonsensical language before its fingers danced along a wall panel beside its head. The noise cut out, and Sandy watched her fingernail drop to the floor. The lizardman glance in her direction before succeeding in doing what she tried and failed to do.

"Alan, do you remember last year's toy line and how we used to make fun of David because he could be one of the girls who danced around the ring holding up the round numbers?" The black cord had just about vanished back into the slab. "You need to do the Jack Moore Metal Fist move on the overgrown canary."

She knew they were running out of time. The other lizardman had also called for help, it was obvious. Alan sat up. He managed to swing his feet over the edge of the slab. The big man got to his feet. He wobbled for a second before steadying himself. The lizardman then pointed at his groaning companion. It wanted her to let it go, to complete the bargain. Sandy pulled it a little closer to the doorway and ran her fingers down the side of the wall. The depression was a still there, but she saw how it reacted. Perhaps some emotions translated between species. It leaned forward a couple of inches. "Wait on, Alan."

Sandy pushed the lizardman's finger into the door release device, shaking her head in annoyance when the gel around its digit solidified. "Oh, you sneaky fucker." She grabbed the injured creature's head and slammed it as hard as she could against the wall, jumping back at the sound of bone cracking.

"That's even worse than having a glass jaw." She stormed up to the remaining lizardman and grabbed its arm, feeling so good when it cringed away. "You're like a weak old man." She grinned at Alan. "If you had smacked this one, I bet your fist would have punched right through its ugly face." The creature let out a quiet gasp. "Oh my! You can understand our language. Tilt your head forward if this is true." She tightened her grip on its arm, as it did as she ordered.

"Well I'll be a monkey's uncle," murmured Alan. He grabbed its other arm and placed it on the wall. "Get us out of here, Mr. Salamander, or I will crush your head." He looked over to the dead creature leaning against the wall. "You see, I don't think you really care what happened to that guy, but I think you do care about your fate. Now do as you're told."

The lizardman chirruped something that Sandy decided was an insult before its claws danced across the wall again. The dead lizardman's finger fell out of the cavity, and the curtains folded back. She hurried out of the room, followed by Alan and his captive. "Bring it over to this doorway, Alan. We might as well make use of it. Saves me from getting gunk on my fingers." Sandy tapped the doorway. "Come on, you know what we want you to do. Open it."

The lizardman chirruped again before pushing its finger into the cavity. Sandy grinned as the curtains folded back. "Alan, you'd better keep hold of both its hands. We don't want it finding another hidden wall panel."

"Got it," he replied.

They found themselves in another identical passageway. She moved over to the wall panel and activated the window, wondering how many others were held captive in this awful place. Sandy choked back a scream when a huge scaly head slammed into the window. Its dagger-sized teeth scraped against the material. She heard a shout of surprise and spun around to find the lizardman had broken free of Alan's grip.

"Stop it!" she yelled.

He tried to grab its arm, but the creature was too fast. She jumped over her friend at exactly the same time when the lizardman's claws danced across a hidden wall panel. A torrent of squeals, growls, and chirps burst from its mouth. Sandy didn't need to know its language to realise that it had locked them in here, and the bastard was laughing at them. To make matters worse, she saw the curtain protecting them and that ferocious dinosaur had begun to fold back.

Sandy wrapped her fingers around the creature's thin wrist. "Laugh this off, pal," she growled. Sandy forced the lizardman's longest finger straight into the solidifying gel, holding it in there while listening to its panicking squawking.

The monster's huge head was already through the widening curtains, the dinosaur's jaw opened and snapped shut, missing the squealing lizardman. It jumped into Sandy. She pushed it away.

"At least it will eat you first. Unless you know how to open these doors."

"How's it going to do that now?" screamed Alan. "You've trapped it in the door mechanism! Oh God. I don't want to die!"

Sandy pulled Alan onto the floor. "We wait until it grabs the lizard then we run into the other room. I bet the others will have the doors open before it finishes eating this guy. Don't worry, Alan! Its pals will be too busy with the dinosaur to bother about us."

The overpowering stench of rotten meat filled the small chamber as the dinosaur roared. She guessed it was getting frustrated at not been able to get to its meal.

Sandy squeezed Alan's hand. She didn't want to die either and certainly didn't want to end up in the guts of some monster that shouldn't even exist anymore. Oh God, it was almost through the door as well! Only its hips were stopping it from charging in here.

Alan shouted something, but the dinosaur's roaring and the lizardman's squeals drowned out his words. It was only when Sandy felt another body fall onto her head when she saw that her plan wasn't going to work. The lizardman had freed itself from the hard gel. She wasn't going anywhere, not with it pinning her to the floor.

Alan hadn't stopped shouting at her. Some of his words had now filtered through the din. He wanted her to turn her head. Sandy arched her back to dislodge the creature and managed to twist her neck a fraction of an inch. It was enough to see the other curtain unfolding, revealing the familiar interior of the home and garden section in the department store.

She took hold of the lizardman's ankle and violently twisted it to the side. The cracking of its bones echoed through the corridor. Sandy fell back and positioned her arms directly under its chest and pushed as hard as she could. It twisted its head back and forth, still screaming. Those screams turned into howls of agony as the dinosaur finally freed its whole body from the doorway and dug its claws into the lizardman's back and pulled it up towards its open mouth.

She gritted her teeth and groaned as the lizardman raked its sharp claws along Sandy's upper arm in a desperate attempt to stay on the ground. She did her best to ignore the throbbing pain coming from the three deep furrows in her flesh. Sandy kept hold of Alan's hand while she scrambled out of the hellish craft.

"It's not following us!" gasped Alan. She could only nod while clutching her wounded arm. Sandy ran past the kettles, pans, and bedding. Screams and shouting came from other parts of the store. None of that was her immediate concern. All she cared about was stopping this bleeding.

## CHAPTER TWELVE

It felt so undignified to be cowering behind the counter in the poncy paper and card store, especially after his incredible escape from the jaws of death, literally. Desmond pushed his thin frame tighter against the wood, trying to ignore the metal handle digging into his back, when he glimpsed the armoured bodies passing the shop.

Once the feathered fuckwits had passed, Desmond scurried out from his hiding place and ran to the back of the store to pick up the sausage roll that he'd dropped in fright when he heard the sound of weapons fire.

He pulled off the plastic wrapper, scrunched it into a tight ball, and pressed the wrapper between the gap between two black fixtures, each displaying neon-coloured card of stupidly expensive prices. Desmond took a big bite of his stolen food while gazing at all the pointless rubbish this place used to flog to the idiots with more money than sense. This was the first time he'd been in here, and it would be the last as well. All the bright colours were giving poor Desmond a right headache. He took another bite and peered around the edge of the fixture, needing to make sure that those terrifying creatures were well and truly gone.

Zinik-Tow hadn't been joking about how scary those bastards looked. The big dinosaurs, the ones with sharp teeth and claws which could slice you into flesh confetti, were bad enough, but at least they had to catch you first. They couldn't dissolve the muscle from your bones from the other side of the frigging mall!

He pushed the last of the sausage roll into his mouth, while contemplating exactly how he was supposed to get back to the safety of the chamber without one of Zinik-Tow's soldier boys turning poor Desmond into a puddle of red treacle. His feathered pal told him the Quantum capsule only stored a dozen of the warrior caste in their stasis tubes, and the squad operated as a single unit commanded by their sergeant. The feathered fuckwit had given the units another name which he couldn't pronounce, but it amounted to pretty much the same thing. Basically, they'd brought along their own version of an assault squad.

"We're all so fucked," he muttered.

He was more annoyed with himself than anyone else. He allowed his self-confidence to get in the way of his natural ability to stay under the radar. His cocky attitude had almost gotten him killed a few minutes ago, all because he fancied a sausage roll. Desmond believed that just because he'd successfully escaped from that time machine, as well as taking out two of their technicians, Old Desmond was practically invulnerable. The king of the mall, the one man who'd be left alive after Zinik-Tow had eliminated every other male on the planet. Oh yeah, he sure did think he was already planet Earth's most valuable human while he strolled down the middle of the concourse, heading straight for Farmdale's Food store. Even the few dinosaurs he saw were avoiding him. Granted, they were too busy munching on the leaves on the Japanese trees to worry about Desmond, but he didn't let that spoil the illusion.

"I really should have listened to that feathered fuckwit a little more closely." He looked down at the bottom of his overalls and rubbed the scorched fabric between his finger and thumb. Desmond had been so close to death. In reality, it was him who'd been the fuckwit.

His new pal had explained their caste system twice to him. He said that for millions of years of strict skill-based segregation, their species had split into five different sub-species, each one bred for their one purpose. Zinik-Tow's sub-species were the only ones able to construct abstract thoughts, who still retained any semblance of free will. His caste ruled over their huge empire.

Sitting there in this stupid shop with sausage roll crumbs down the front of his overalls, Desmond had no problem in reciting his pal's words as well as the hidden meaning. Yet back then, just after he'd snapped the neck of that yellow flamingo, Desmond thought he was fucking superman. All he'd done was to kill one of their technicians, some poor guy who was about as scary as a five-year-old kiddie.

The sound of them firing those scary guns reached him. Desmond moaned quietly as the delayed shock hit him like an express train. He rolled into a tight ball and closed his eyes, listening to the shouts, screams, and hoarse shrieks coming from his fellow humans as those monsters, clad in that iridescent armour plating, melted them. Those two-legged tanks were unstoppable. His pal's dream was in ruins. Not even he would be able to withstand that devastating firepower. Desmond opened one eye.

Zinik-Tow might already be dead for all he knew. It's not like poor Desmond had any way of knowing. It meant that he had a very important decision to make. There was no way he'd be able to get down to the level under this one without bumping into either another dino, eager to feast on his bones or those soldiers, currently turning every other human into scotch broth. It wouldn't take him any longer than ten minutes to make it to the mall's carpark, though, and as the soldiers have just come from that direction, as long as the pool of scarlet goop wasn't acidic, he should be able to be home and dry without anything else nasty happening to him. Hell, there wasn't anything stopping him from popping into Farmdale's again to grab that other sausage roll. It's not like anybody else was going to eat it.

It's not like he was running away or betraying his new pal. It was just survival, plain and simple. Anyway, it's only what Zinik-Tow did to him in that timeship. He abandoned Desmond, not giving a shit what happened to him. He slowly got to his feet and slowly made his way over to the counter, keeping his eyes fixed on the glass front. Then again, if Zinik-Tow had taken poor Desmond with him, he might be as dead as the feathered fuckwit as well.

He made doubly sure that nothing moved on the concourse before venturing from the safety of the store. There would be no strutting about like some proud peacock for this downtrodden janitor anymore.

Something metallic clattered onto the tiles. Desmond jumped back into the shop and hid behind the counter. It was a full minute of silence before he dared to move again. Desmond found a shaky grin spreading over his face at the sight of a very expensive wristwatch lying close to the glass front.

The tattered and burnt fabric in front of the photobooth gave Desmond a pretty good indication as to what must have happened. He walked over to the booth, wincing at the acrid smell drifting out from the interior. Steeling himself, Desmond pulled the curtain back. Under a pile of smouldering clothing, he saw a few blackened bones swimming in a thick, red lumpy soup. He placed the palm of his hand against the glass plate in front of the red plastic stool, trying to comprehend the God-challenging power which those creatures possessed.

He knew that none of those moving nightmares had passed by his shop, meaning they had just pointed their gun at the back of this booth and fired. Its magic ray gun beam had passed straight through metal, plastic, and glass before reducing this clown into goop and bone.

Desmond would have loved to have a play with one of those gizmos. Zinik-Tow had told him about the magnificent Saurion Empire, about how they had conquered dozens of planets, about every species they encountered who fell beneath their feet within days. Desmond thought the feathered fuckwit was just blowing his own trumpet, having a bit of a pissing contest with this poor janitor. After seeing the power of one of those weapons though, Desmond now understood exactly how fucked the humans were going to be once these monsters left this mall.

The sound of weapons' fire grew distant. Desmond figured they'd be running out of people to melt pretty soon. Not that he cared, his future lay in the opposite direction, towards the carpark and freedom. Also, another sausage roll. He looked down the middle of the concourse, seeing the devastation left by those reptilian soldiers. If he did make a break for it, then it's likely that sometime in the future, there was a good chance that he'd be meeting a similar fate as *Mr. Melty* in the photobooth. Zinik-Tow had also told him that the current thinking in the higher ranks of the Sauron high command was that the only way to ensure total dominance would be to eliminate all traces of the conquered species, to literally melt them off the planet.

Desmond didn't want to be melted. He wanted to live. He wanted to prove to everybody that he wasn't some piece of dirt, only fit for menial tasks to be talked down to and bossed about. He wanted all of that, but more than anything, he wanted that hot chick from the beauty parlour. Desmond wanted to make her his queen.

None of his dreams would be happening if he did run away like a frightened mouse. There really was no other choice. He couldn't leave the mall until he was sure that his new pal really was dead. It was that simple. There was also the small matter of rescuing Sandy. Oh sure, she had brushed him off the first time. By now, after seeing the danger out here, she was bound to be a little more compliant; especially when she learns that he's going to be risking his life to save her sorry arse.

With his goal now clear, Desmond waved goodbye to that sausage roll and slowly walked along the concourse, staying close to the shops. He knew the glass and concrete wouldn't save him if the fuckwits saw him, but he counted on them being too busy with all the fun stuff to murder in front of them to be bothered about their back. After all, who'd be stupid enough to follow those killing machines?

He grinned to himself. No, not stupid, just sneaky. "As cunning as a fox," he whispered, finally seeing their shadows as the soldiers left a console game shop at the other end of the mall. It looked like they were heading back towards that timeship. This put him in an awkward position. If the hot chick was still locked up in there, she wouldn't stand a chance against those things. Yet Desmond's route took him past in the other direction, towards the stairs leading down to the lower level.

He leaned against a jeweller's shop, gazing at the display of expensive necklaces. His hot chick would look fantastic in the gold number right at the back, the one that would take him almost a year's worth of salary to buy.

The soldiers were now close to a herd of four-legged dinosaurs, similar to the ones he passed earlier. Did these guys have an infinite supply of these buggers? More to the point, how the bloody hell had they escaped? He'd been inside that freaky place and everything was locked as tight as a drum.

It didn't look like the soldiers were going to be doing anything else apart from standing about, so he decided to have a look inside the shop. Desmond remembered how he felt in their timeship and how distance felt completely different. That ship of theirs wasn't much bigger than a couple of articulated trucks side by side. Yet, Desmond knew that even if all the dinosaurs that he'd seen so far were squashed up like sardines, only about half of them would fit inside.

Desmond reached into the shop display, snagged the necklace, and stuffed it into his pocket. Thinking about physics and all that time-travelling nonsense made his head hurt, so he let it slide and went with the flow instead. It sounded like a better deal than thinking about the impossible.

He left the shop and gazed across at the soldiers, seeing that there had been a reason for their break in the marching after all. Two of them had caught one of the dinosaurs. They each had a hind leg and were pulling in the opposite direction. The others seemed to find this hilarious. The trapped animal couldn't cry out because another soldier had its huge paws clamped around the animal's mouth.

Incredibly, the other animals in the herd carried on chomping on the foliage. Desmond thought they would have galloped away at least. Then again, why should they? It's not like there was that much growing plant-life in the shopping centre. The bits of greenery must be like an oasis for the buggers. As long as the soldiers only killed one of their kind, the others would be safe.

One of the legs was wrenched out of the hip-joint. The other soldier had to twist the other leg and jerk it backwards before that one was pulled from the bleeding torso. The one holding the mouth slammed its other paw down on the animal's head. Desmond heard the skull-shattering hammer blow from where he stood. It then ripped away its jaw, pulled off the tongue, and took a huge bite out of it.

The others kneeled around the carcass and used their claws to rip through the hide to get at the steaming meat. The only ones not joining in were the two soldiers holding those hind legs. They both took bites from their prize at the same time while watching the mall. They must be their lookouts. That made sense too. He'd seen those nature documentaries in Africa and what happened when a lion took down a zebra.

Desmond guessed that this must be their equivalent of stopping at the eatery. It did make him wonder what Zinik-Tow did for food. It would be the ultimate irony if Desmond did find the feathered fuckwit alive only to discover further down the line that he was saving this poor janitor for breakfast.

He wasn't the only one watching this feast. Their lookouts might not see them, but Desmond sure did. From this distance, he couldn't make out their faces, but he wasn't the only human still alive on the level. They darted out from behind an escalator only to disappear again when the two lookout soldiers gazed into the department store. It gave him hope that perhaps his Sandy had made it out of that timeship after all. If anyone could have escaped, it would be her. She was an untamed spirit, the perfect mate for him.

The people he noticed in the department store weren't the only ones interested in what the soldiers were doing either. Three small dinosaurs had managed to conceal themselves close to the herd of plant-eating dinosaurs. These were meat-eaters. In fact, they looked very much like Zinik-Tow's pet. The herd didn't seem all that bothered by their presence either. From the way the soldiers were behaving, they had seen the new arrivals and didn't care about their presence, or hadn't noticed them.

He took out the necklace and held it above his head, watching the mall's soft lighting reflect off the gems. Sandy was going to love this. It would be his peace offering to show that he did care about her. He sniffed and shoved the necklace back into his pocket. Not that she'd have much of a choice in the matter. Once Zinik-Tow had finished putting every other human male down, there wouldn't be anyone left for her anyway.

The three meat-eaters literally leaped over the grazing herd, each one landing on a soldier's head. He shook his head in utter disbelief as their snapping jaws tried and failed to bite through the soldier's protective head coverings. It struck Desmond as such a strange thing for them to do, considering they ignored the huge carcass. Did they know their attack would be a futile gesture? One soldier grabbed a tail and pulled it off its head. The soldier held it by the hips and slammed its body into the floor. One of the other small meat-eaters had fared even worse. A mushed-up mess of skull and brain was all that remained of its head. The tiny fact that its attacker was already dead couldn't have reached the soldier's brain as it continued to stamp the meat-eater into the ground.

Only one was able to leave the soldier's impromptu rest area alive. It limped away from them, occasionally turning its head to spit at the laughing soldiers. One of the lookouts dropped the severed leg, aimed his big gun at the retreating animal, and fired. His laughing increased as the meat-eater's body dissolved.

That had to be the weirdest thing he'd seen so far. What had possessed those things to commit suicide? They weren't stupid. Desmond had already seen that those little monsters had more brains than those plant-eaters. "It must be hate," he surmised. "Or fear." He tried to remember if Zinik-Tow had said anything about having anything like those animals in his alternate time-frame. Something told Desmond that in their time-frame they had no animals at all on the planet. That made sense, considering how much respect for life that they'd shown so far.

He watched the commander berate his two lookouts. It pulled the hind legs out of their grasps and threw the meat over to the other soldiers before he pulled something from his side. His took two steps back while the lookouts bunched together. The commander then aimed the small device at the pair. Desmond leaned forward, hoping it was going to turn the pair of those lookouts into puddles of slime.

The commander fired. Desmond shook his head in disgust when all they did was fall to the floor and writhe about in the blood while screaming in agony. If he'd have been that commander, he would have killed them both, just to teach others a lesson.

After a few more seconds, the lookouts got to their knees, and threw up before getting back onto their feet. The others crowded around the lookouts. From where Desmond stood, it looked like they were helping them get themselves sorted out as their commander silently watched over them. It almost brought a tear to Desmond's eyes, watching how they acted together.

It brought back the memories of his short stint in the forces. For the first time in Desmond's crappy life, he had been happy. Oh, just like his family, they too the rip out of him. Unlike those of his blood, his army buddies would watch his back. They looked after each other. They were his true family.

Judging from the reactions of the other soldiers, Desmond guessed that they were surprised as him to find their two lookouts still breathing. He didn't think it was the sudden spurt of sentimentality on the commander's front. It was more of the simple fact that those soldiers were an endangered species now. Once they were gone, that was it, no more biological tanks. Just like the rest of the feathered fuckwits and the dinosaurs, they were stuck here. There was no going back home.

The soldiers reformed their squad and continued on their way, disappearing into the department store. It didn't take long before the familiar sound of weapons' fire reached him. Desmond left the store's alcove and made his way other to the over side of the concourse, keeping his eyes fixed on the entrance to the department store. It would be just his misfortune to have one of those soldiers turning around at exactly the same time as he passed the store. If that happened, it would be *goodbye* to Desmond. Unlike those lookouts, he wouldn't get a second chance.

His luck had held out so far. And he wanted it to stay that way as well. Desmond reached the scene of the slaughter and eased his way past the animals still grazing on what was left of the vegetation. He heard screams and shouts coming from the department store, but just like these four-legged beasts, it had nothing to do with him. Desmond didn't care who those soldiers melted. He knew for a fact that if the shoe had been on the other foot, none of those idiots would give two shits about him.

The door leading to the lower level was within sight now. He skidded to a halt just before he reached the mall's restaurant area and watched a couple of smaller dinosaurs as they climbed on top of a large carcass. A brown one with a long neck pulled off a strip of meat and attempted to swallow its prize, only to find another, slightly larger animal had sunk its teeth into its tail. They snapped at each other for a moment before a large roar, coming from somewhere else on this level, scared them away.

Desmond felt the hairs on the back of his neck stand on end when he heard that noise. So far, he hadn't had the dubious pleasure of bumping into anything much larger than him yet, and he intended it to stay that way. He gave it another few more seconds before he ran past the carcass, almost jumping out of his skin when the dinosaur that he thought had fled hissed at him from inside the dead animal's ribcage.

"Bugger off," he muttered. "I'm not interested in stealing your food." Desmond got to those double doors without getting his arse bitten. "I must have some Irish in me." He grinned, reaching for the door.

Two pairs of hands whipped out and fastened around Desmond's wrists as soon as he pushed the doors opens. He yelped in shock and found himself gazing into the furious faces of the mall manager and one of the security guards.

"Fancy meeting you here," said Mrs. Killmore. She turned to the guard. "What do you think we should do with him, Mo?"

Desmond tried to struggle out of their grip and received a sharp slap across his cheek for his trouble.

"Do that again, you little shit," she growled, "and I'll punch you in the balls. Now stay still."

"Get off me! I haven't done anything to you!" This was so unfair. Why were they doing this? Desmond so wished his pal was here. He'd soon fix their wagon. He did think of using him to threaten them but backed out at the last minute. The furious looks on their faces told him that his association with the feathered fuckwit was probably why they were acting like this.

"He's a turncoat. A traitor to his own kind." Mo straightened his ripped black jacket. "If this was war, then we'd have to execute him."

The woman turned around, and then Desmond saw that these two were not alone. Another five people were standing on the landing twelve steps below them. He didn't recognise any of them. He guessed they must be what remained of the shoppers. Desmond tried to smile without snarling. "Please, I'm just like you lot, trying to stay alive. I haven't hurt anyone." He swallowed a couple of times, trying to dislodge the lump that had appeared at the back of his throat. Was he appealing to their sense of good nature?

"I saw him with one of them," shouted a young blonde girl. Tears poured down her cheek. "He stood there and grinned when those evil bastards let the dinosaur rip my Jeremy apart. I say we do the same to him."

The others nodded in unison.

"Seems fair to me," said Mrs. Killmore. "Desmond, I have never liked you anyway. There's been more complaints about your attitude than anybody else in the mall. I was going to let you go in a few days' time anyway. Looks like I won't have to now."

"What do you want done with him?"

"We'll throw him off the balcony, Mo. The fall won't kill him, but it should break his legs. We can then all watch as the dinosaurs pull him apart."

Desmond's screams were cut short when the security guard clamped his hand over the man's mouth.

## CHAPTER THIRTEEN

Jefferson wrapped the bandage around Sandy's arm one last time before tying it. "That should do it," he announced. Janine had already removed the girl's previous bandage, a blood-soaked strip of blouse, and popped it into a plastic bag. Jefferson thought she was just being generally neat and tidy, the way women are, until it twigged that she'd done it to stop the predators from catching their scent. Considering that he was now down to just three bolts, they needed to take every precaution.

"He'd make a great nurse," said David. "Seriously. I reckon we should all put together and buy Jeffdude one of those sexy numbers, complete with black stockings and everything." He winked at Alan.

"And to think I was actually missing the idiot," muttered Sandy. She smiled at Jefferson. "Thanks for fixing me up, by the way."

"No problem. Alan did a good job on the first one."

"Do you think it could be infected? I mean, you reckon I should grab some antibiotics or something?"

Jefferson shook his head. "I think that's only for bites, Sandy. I guess if you start to see any pus coming out of the wounds then we can see if we can find some. We were always told to seek medical attention in a case like that. Our first aid course only covered the basics." He looked over at the store front, noticing more activity. He heard some shouting as well as more movement. "I think we should move away from the entrance."

Janine passed the plastic bag to David, then hurried over to one of the stone pillars and peered around it. She looked back at Jefferson. She didn't look at all happy at what she'd just seen. He grabbed his crossbow and motioned Sandy, David, and Alan to move back.

He ran over to her position, a bolt already notched. "Oh shit."

Jefferson had gleaned everything he could from Sandy's adventure in the nightmarish place. A job made all the more difficult with David's constant interruptions. It was like he didn't even care about the trauma that his friends had been through. He acted like some excitable child, wanting to know every detail of everything they'd seen in there. In the end, Alan had to take him aside before Sandy knocked him out. The only time when he'd stopped talking was when Sandy first described the creatures.

"They don't look like what attacked Sandy."

He shook his head. "No, something tells me that we're in more trouble than we even realised." Jefferson saw a similarity to Sandy's stick-like yellow bird men but only superficially. It was like comparing a dwarf giraffe with a two-legged rhino, wearing a suit of armour and carrying a gun the size of a lamp stand.

They looked a bit like the armoured soldiers they sold in the Gaming Warbox store on the level below. David had loads of the things in his bedroom, all painted up and posed on a model battlefield. He sighed, so wishing that everything was back as it should be. Jefferson didn't think he could take anymore of this bullshit. To think that just a few hours ago, he'd been craving for some excitement in his life.

Janine took his hand. "We'd better go join the others," she whispered.

He wondered if it was possible to wish everything back to how it was, with perhaps a couple of changes. Jefferson didn't want to lose Janine, that's for sure. "It looks like we're going to have to find another way downstairs. We won't be able to get past those things." They stopped beside a herd of grazing dinosaurs. "We can't fight them. I know that much."

His crossbow wouldn't be any use against those things. Janine was right, they should go back before those armoured rhinos came in here. Right now, though, it looked like they were having too much fun torturing one of those poor dinosaurs to bother coming in here. Jefferson didn't think that would last long. The quicker they were out of here, the better.

He looked back at the others. Alan sat on the floor with David and Sandy crouching beside the man. God, he looked terrible. He hadn't been right ever since they had stumbled upon Sandy and Alan. Then again, after what Sandy had told Jefferson what they'd been through in that place, it didn't surprise him. Alan had never been the most robust of individuals.

Janine pulled him away from the pillar just as those armoured monsters had grabbed one of the plant-eaters. Jefferson didn't even want to think what they'd do to the poor thing. He twiddled with his crossbow, that feeling of being helpless reappeared. Oh God. He so wanted to get out of here.

"What is it? What did you see?"

"You know your collection of Star Marines, those few stupid plastic soldiers on your top shelf?"

David nodded. "Two shelves now, Jeffdude. I bought two full battalions of Space-cluster Judgmentors from eBay a couple of weeks ago."

"Yeah well, that's who's now outside the shop."

Both Sandy and Janine grabbed an arm each when David tried to rush past him. "This isn't a game, you fucking idiot," hissed Jefferson. "Those things are real and will so enjoy pulling off your arms and legs." He could now hear their deep booming noises. Whatever they were doing, it was keeping them out of the store. "You okay, Alan?"

The other man raised his head a couple of inches. "Sure, just tired, that's all." He glanced over at David. "That guy's annoying enough to sap the life out of anyone."

The man's poor attempt at humour wasn't fooling Jefferson. He could see there was something wrong with him. He walked over to where Alan sat and gently pulled him up. He frowned; the guy's skin felt weird, like it was slipping around his bones. "We'll be out of here really soon now, dude. Just a little longer."

"We can go through the back of the store," said Janine. "This place shares a staff toilet with the phone shop next door." She kept a firm grip on David's arm while moving over to Jefferson. "Is your other friend going to be okay?"

Jefferson looked over at Alan. He'd been asking himself the same question. He so wanted to put the lad's pale complexion and his inactivity down to shock, but it was more that. He really did look ill. Right now though, there wasn't anything he could do about him, apart from getting the poor bugger out of here as quickly as he could.

"It's okay, Jefferson," said Sandy. "I'll grab him." She nodded at the crossbow. "We need you to watch our backs."

"Like this will make a difference," he muttered. Jefferson waited for his friends to hurry past him before taking up the rear. Those armoured things really disturbed him, even more than everything that had happened to them. He had just seen the beginnings of an army. From the brief glimpses, Jefferson guessed that nothing his species possessed would be of any use against them. Jefferson might be wrong; he could be allowing his natural disposition to worry about everything and anything get the better of him. None of them were acting right. David was being more of a cock than normal. From what Sandy had told him, and with his own eyes, she had turned into a frigging warrior ninja.

It had to be shock. Alan might be at home in a high-stress environment but only when the stress came from managing staff holiday rotas, organising stock replenishment schedules, and ensuring the product planning sheets adhered to the parent company's regulations. At no time did his job description include battling dinosaurs or escaping from something that belonged in a crappy science fiction movie.

He put his troubled thoughts away and focussed on the task at hand, namely getting him and his friends out of here in one piece. Thankfully, the predators were now very few. They had heard their roars and growls in the distance, but they were now few and far between. He guessed they must have either eaten each other or gone in search for more prey. Jefferson skirted past a chewed-up human skeleton. There was also the possibility that the bastards had all gone to find somewhere to sleep off their meals of plant-eating dinosaurs with a side dish of terrified shopper.

If that really was the case, the need to get out of here only became more urgent. There wasn't many of them left now. He had seen glimpses of other humans but that was more scarce than hearing the meat-eaters.

Janine stopped beside a plain white door. She tapped the security combination lock on the side. "I have a friend who works in the department store. Thankfully, this is one of the days when she doesn't work." The woman tapped in a six-digit code, turned the metal handle to the side, and then pulled open the door. "Come on, we'll be safe in here. I'm not really supposed to know the code, but I don't really think that matters anymore."

Jefferson waited until everybody else was inside before he let the door close. It wasn't much different from his shop's staff area, just better equipped. For a start, they had their own vending machine and a canteen. Gloria would have loved it in here. Bloody hell! He hadn't given that woman a moment's thought until now. "David, any idea what happened to Gloria?"

His friend shook his head. David helped himself to a bowl of biscuits left on one of the tables. "Not a clue. To be honest, I was kinda surprised that she wasn't still behind her till when we nicked that set of tools earlier." He pushed one of the biscuits in his mouth. "Knowing her, she probably hasn't even noticed the bleeding dinosaurs."

A bit of a cruel assessment of their co-worker, but he had a point. Nothing ever phased Gloria. It seemed like an age since they had all sat around that table, listening to David bang on about him taking down that shoplifter. In truth, it had been Gloria who had collared him first and pushed the guy towards the exit. David's only contribution had been to panic when Gloria told him to keep an eye on the guy while she went on her break.

Janine gave him a kiss before she left them in the canteen while she scouted out the route. She pointed to the sword when he asked her if she wanted him to go with her. Jefferson watched her leave before he too snatched a biscuit. He wanted to laugh when he saw the clock mounted on the wall above the microwave. According to that, their shop would be closing in about five minutes. He looked at the biscuit before dropping in back in the dish. Like there was anything remotely funny about their situation. He kept saying to himself that everything was going to be all right once they left the mall, *if* they left the mall, that is. Yet, according to that clock, he'd been in here for over four hours, witnessing all this senseless death, running from animals that should be fucking extinct, and now they were hiding from huge rhino-sized bastard lizards!

He turned around and placed his forehead against the cold wall. To top it all, to make this situation even worse than it already was, Jefferson firmly believed that there wasn't going to be any help from beyond the mall. He slowly spun around and watched the others. David was still eating those bloody biscuits. Sandy had sat down next to David and was running her fingers up and down the bandage, while Alan sat on a wooden chair in the far corner of the room. He looked to be sleeping.

After four hours, this place should be overrun with police and ambulances. He then remembered the pissing dinosaurs. And David's star bollocks marines. No, scrap the coppers. The army should be in here by now. They weren't, so something else must have happened somewhere else. It was bloody obvious. All this must be happening in the other large buildings across the city, or even across the country. They could be in the middle of a full-scale invasion.

Jefferson closed his eyes and silently counted to ten. It shouldn't come as any surprise to find himself going through the stages of shock about now, and why not? According to Janine, only the department store's employees could come in here, meaning this place was safe. He didn't even think the rhino soldiers would bother trying to get through that door either. An ideal place for him to have his little breakdown.

There was some kind of commotion going on in the background. As he could only hear Sandy's voice, he put it down to David acting up again. What else could it be? After all, they were all safe now. Jefferson slid down to the floor and put his hands over his ears to block out the noise. His legs had started to shake. It wouldn't be long for the rest of his body to follow suit. Jefferson wished Gloria was here right now. She'd tell him a couple of silly jokes, make him drink some warm tea, and generally take the mickey out of David.

Gloria wasn't here, though. His Janine was around somewhere. *His Janine*. Those words sounded like they were made for each other. Perhaps something good had come out of this clusterfuck after all.

Even through the improvised ear protection, her voice still penetrated his brain. What happened to keeping quiet until Janine came back? It then dawned on him that it was Janine's voice he could hear.

He snapped open his eyes. Both women stood in front of David. He was still stuffing those biscuits down his throat. Their formless words made no sense, but their gestures were all too familiar. Both women were terrified. Sandy pointed to the corner while Janine looked over towards where Janine said they'd be able to escape to.

Her eyes then found his, and Jefferson's *fly on the wall* situation abruptly vanished when she ran over to him and pulled him onto his feet.

"We have a problem," she said, dragging Jefferson over to the door. Both David and Sandy were over by Alan now. She was shaking Alan's knee while his other friend stood at a safe distance wringing his hands. None of them seemed all that bothered about Janine's anguished state.

She opened the door and pulled him through.

"What's wrong with Alan?"

"I'm not so sure," she replied. "Sandy said he hadn't been great ever since their escape." She then spun around and grabbed his shoulders. "Jefferson, we really are in big trouble here."

The woman moved to the side.

"Take a look. Just don't let them see you."

He peered through the small square window cut into the door. Jefferson whirled around, so wishing what Janine had just told him wasn't true. He walked over to the wall and gazed at a poster displaying three smiling women, each one wearing a Martin's Department Store uniform, each one proudly holding a customer service medal.

Those poor bits of people he'd just glimpsed on the other side of that door wore the same uniforms. Their killers were still in there, picking off bits of meat from exposed bone. Jefferson wanted to close his eyes but daren't, as that image of all those teeth, claws, and bright feathers feasting on those people had been burnt into his retina.

"I didn't want to see that," he gasped, feeling his guts performing a slow roll.

Jefferson's head then smacked into the wall when Janine slapped her hand hard across his cheek. Before he could even catch his breath, the woman followed her sudden bout of unprovoked violence by wrapping her arms around his waist and kissing him deeply.

"I love you, Jefferson," she said, after she'd pulled away. "And that is something that I never thought I'd say again." Janine sighed. "I shouldn't have left you in there alone. You thought you were safe in there, that the monsters wouldn't be able to get you. Your adrenalin level began to normalise."

"I'm sorry, but I really have no idea what you are talking about," he said, rubbing his cheek. Jefferson placed both his hands on her neck. "I won't complain if you kiss me again, though."

"When all this is over, honey, we'll do much more than just kiss. Right now, I need you to be alert, to have that fear of impending death right there." Janine tapped his forehead. "You were going into shock. You'd found your safe place and were about to crawl into it."

"What are we going to do about getting out of here?" Jefferson knew he had three bolts left and figured the single sword they had left might take out another two. Would that be enough to make them panic and run off? He thought of the little dinos back in the eatery. There were loads of those things but the ones in there were three times the size.

"We have three choices. We stay in here and wait for the dinosaurs to leave. We try to fight them, or we wait for those huge armoured living trucks to leave." She stroked the back of his hands. "Your shaking has stopped. That's good. Are you ready for round two?"

"I guess. How did you know? And why didn't the others...?"

"Why didn't the others notice?" she finished off. "We're the civilians of modern Western consumerism, that's why. We are not supposed to be thrust into situations of not knowing whether our next moment will be our last one." She smiled and kissed him again. "That speech came straight from the bible of my late husband. He loved that particular statement. He had plenty more just like it. I tell you, Trevor would have adored being in here with all this lot. Well, he would as long as he had his trusty assault rifle with unlimited ammunition." She took his hand. "Come on, we'd better go join the others. I don't want them to think that we have run out and left them here."

He nodded, realising that she'd just said that she loved him. Apart from just finding out she was once married and she had a couple of kids, he knew next to nothing about her. As they approached the door, he imagined him and Janine sitting in one of the restaurants in the mall after all this was over. Holding hands and grinning at each other, not having to speak, just thankful they were still alive. Jefferson hoped Alan wouldn't be too pissed if he asked David to be his best man at their wedding.

"Is it safe?"

Jefferson shook his head. "We don't stand a chance of getting out that way, David. The next room is clogged with meat-eaters."

"What kind are they?"

His hackles went straight up, but after a couple of seconds, it became clear that David's question had just been instinctive. His mind was elsewhere. It scared Jefferson a lot to see David actually looking anxious. He saw why.

Alan had not moved from his spot. He looked so close to death. Jefferson ran over to the lad and skidded to a halt when he saw how much he had deteriorated in only a couple of minutes. What the hell was this? The poor lad's flesh looked like it was getting ready to melt off his bones. He gazed into Sandy's tear-streaked face. She gently held Alan's hand.

"I remember one of them lifting up my arm," whispered Alan. He ran his tongue over his lips, before bursting into a fit of coughing. "God, that hurts." He lifted his head. "I fucked up, Jeff. Sorry for spoiling your day."

"What is it? What's wrong with him?"

Jefferson pulled David back over to the table. "I don't know, man."

"Jeff. Will you tell Chris that I love him?"

"Bollocks, mate. You can tell him that yourself."

"I think they did something to both of us," said Sandy. "Oh God, yeah, I remember now!" her breath came out in shuddering jerks. "They held this silver tube over my stomach. I screamed as this dirty green light came out of the end. I thought they were going to burn me, but it felt cold. So cold." Sandy looked over at David and Jefferson. "Guys, it might be a better idea if you leave us here. If we're infected, there's no telling what we have."

Jefferson shook his head. "No way. Not a chance. I'm not leaving the pair of you." Janine crouched beside Alan.

"There's a doctor's surgery a short walk from the shopping centre. As soon as we're clear, I'll run across and bring someone over. We just need you to hang on for a bit longer." She nodded over at the other door. "Jefferson, why don't you see if those living trucks have gone?"

"I'll do it," cried David, running over to the door.

"Jefferson, grab him!" cried Sandy. "He's going to run out on us."

He raced after his mate, knowing that Sandy wasn't wrong. He heard that tone as well. The bloody fool was going to get himself and the rest of them killed. Jefferson pushed through the door and saw him streaking along the wall, heading for the far end of the store. He wasn't the only one who'd noticed him either. Every single one of the fearsome grotesque soldiers had spotted David, and they moved in the intercept. Jefferson gasped when he saw their speed.

David was fast, but he certainly wasn't as fast as those armour-plated monsters. He must have seen that he wouldn't stand a chance of dodging past them and had spun around, now running straight for Jefferson. Oh fuck, David was leading those bastards straight for him! He turned and ran back to the door, knowing that they had no choice now but to chance those carnivorous dinosaurs.

Jefferson stopped dead when the door opened before he could reach it and the others all stepped out into the store. Both girls were carrying Alan between them. "What are you doing?" he shrieked. "Those things are right behind us!"

"Grab that idiot!" said Janine. "Come on, do it, there's not much time left."

He saw those huge things thundering towards them, their strange-looking guns already trained on their heads. David tried to run past Jefferson. He kicked out his feet, knocking the lad onto the floor. Sandy reached down and wrapped her fingers around his ankle.

"Your turn," Jefferson. "Take my hand."

The soldiers slowed and stopped. They formed a semi-circle around the humans; their weapons still trained on Jefferson's body. His fingers managed to find the hand of the woman he loved, while he forced himself from curling up in hysterical laughter. Like any of those things needed a weapon to obliterate any of his group! They were larger than black bears, with teeth to make a crocodile weep. Thick iridescent-studded armour covered most of their feathered bodies, leaving only their heads and ankles showing. Jefferson had seen what remained of that plant-eating dinosaur, and from the amount of blood staining their huge paws, he knew that they must have literally torn it apart.

Jefferson tightened his grip on Janine's hand. He closed his eyes and waited for these monsters to do the same to him and his friends.

## CHAPTER FOURTEEN

Mo and Mrs. Killmore had dragged him down the first flight of stairs. Desmond's first attempt to escape had been thwarted by Mo by slamming his knee between Desmond's legs when he tried to sink his teeth into the woman's arm.

Between the tears, sobbing, and the throbbing pain in his balls, he watched how the others not holding this poor janitor cleared a path through a pack of scavenging dinosaurs at the bottom of the stairwell by spraying them with a combination of air freshener, furniture polish, and deodorant. The little brown dinosaurs stayed in the shadows, hissing and growling while the group tentatively stepped over the pieces of chewed-up plant-eating dinosaur. Desmond thought it now smelled like a summer meadow crossed with a teen's bedroom before they go out on the pull.

Those dinosaurs waited until they were a good few paces away from their prize before they emerged from under the stairs. It wasn't fair. Why hadn't they attacked them? He counted eleven of them. That was enough to take out both Mo and the horrible lesbian. Desmond wasn't all that bothered about the others. He'd be able to sort out those losers. What were they going to do, spray him to death?

The pair of them had taken an arm each and were dragging his body along the concourse. Neither Mo nor Mrs. Killmore had said a word since they had caught him. They hadn't even explained why the sudden change of plan, why they were on the ground floor instead of the level above. Desmond looked up at the balconies about twenty feet up and decided not to pursue that line of questioning any further, in case they did change their mind.

Once the worst of the pain had turned into a dull throbbing, Desmond had tried everything to get them to let him go. Everything from how they were turning themselves into a target to continuous screaming, with the hope of attracting those soldiers. He'd only stopped doing that when Mo savagely twisted his arm behind him back. Desmond had screamed then but for a different reason. The only tactic that he hadn't tried was to threaten them with Desmond's new pal. Something told him though, that if this poor janitor did go down that road, they'd likely stop dragging him to wherever and just kick him to death right here and now, next to this kiddie ride. He did not want to die laying next to a bright pink plastic bus. This level now looked like an abattoir. Desmond dreaded to think of how many people must have died down here. This was worse than the level above them. His two captors dragged Desmond past dozens of mutilated bodies, both dinosaur and human. He wasn't the only one to be affected by all this devastation either.

One of the others in the group, a dark-haired man who was carrying his can of air freshener like it was a rocket launcher, skidded to a halt in front on a couple of dead kids. He muttered something about all this being such a *senseless waste of lives*, while he wiped the tears away from his eyes.

The corpses were slumped in front of the shoe shop, their heads lying on their chests. He knew why this sentimental idiot was blubbering like a big baby. Judging from the tightly clasped hands, these two were lovers. Desmond imagined that the lad would have been putting up with the annoying cow going into every stupid girly shop and sighing over all the brightly coloured crap just so he'd be able to get a jump later on. It sounded harsh, but it was true. Desmond had seen the behaviour dozens of times while cleaning up the shopping centre. The predators had eaten their way up their legs, stopping once they reached their thighs. He guessed the dinosaurs which did this had spied another meal. It was a shitty way to die, but at least they died together.

All the others were now bowing their heads. Two of his captors were even saying a prayer. He knew for a fact that none of them would be saying a prayer over his body. Not that they were going to get a chance of doing the deed. He'd think of something to stop them.

Desmond turned his head and coughed. They all looked up and glared at him. That was fine, let them glare, he'd fix all their wagons. Right now though, he needed to be calm and clever. He stared back at the middle-aged man, trying to look sincere. "You can stop this! You can stop any more senseless waste from happening. Just tell them to let me go."

"Bollocks! This is all your fault in the first place," he snarled. "These poor people died because you cosied up to the enemy." He marched over to Desmond and lowered his face until he was just a hair's breath away from the man's nose. "You're a collaborator, a fifth columnist. Hell, you're not even that. All you are is some dirty scumbag who'd do anything to save his own worthless hide, even if it means watching the rest of his species die."

God, where did all this anger come from? The guy obviously had problems. He jerked his head back, so he didn't have to cope with this madman's peppermint breath. "Okay, I'll admit that I might have made a couple of dumb mistakes. What do you expect? I mean, just look around you. I was scared, okay? Come on, admit it. We've all made mistakes. It doesn't mean we should be put to death. Hell, you're making a mistake right now. Come on, I'd be on my knees if I could. Stop this now. This doesn't justify a revenge killing. It isn't even that. This is cold-blooded murder, plain and simple."

"Are you done, Desmond?" inquired the mall manager. "We want to get on."

Desmond glared at the woman holding his arm. He so wanted to bite off her nose. "You need to think about what you're doing! You'll all be sent to jail for this. The police will be here any second. Stop this madness before it's too late."

Mo laughed. "Yeah right, like anybody's going to turn up. Even if they did, who's going to tell them, Desmond? You'll be dead in another few minutes, and we won't be saying anything."

This so wasn't fair. Desmond hadn't done anything wrong. He certainly didn't deserve whatever fate these maniacs had in store for this poor janitor. The security did have a point, though. They would get away with killing him.

Zinik-Tow had already informed him that the hairless vermin infecting this planet would be too distracted with other events to care about the misfortunes of the last few survivors within this building. Apart from saying that his great enemy's plan was now unfolding, he refused to elaborate. After what Desmond had seen so far, he doubted that the bastards would be organising a charity gala.

Even if by some miracle somebody did get in here, how long would they last before the rampaging dinosaurs ate them or the soldiers on the next level turned Desmond's rescuers into horse glue?

Desmond lunged for the bitch's face, but her reaction was far too attuned. His snapping jaw clacked on fresh air and he ended up with a tight fist crashing into the side of his head.

"Do that again, you little shit, and I'll—"

"You'll do what, you fat cow?" he spat. "How can you make it any worse?"

Mo stopped and grinned at Mrs. Killmore. "I know you said you wanted to feed him to the dinosaur in the furniture shop, but maybe we should do this ourselves."

"Mo, I thought we had already decided that throwing him off the balcony would be too quick."

"I know that, it's just I thought we shouldn't let something else do the job for us. I thought that maybe we should grab some sharp knives and slice him up a bit. You know, like one slice for every poor sod who's died because of him."

The middle-aged aged man nodded eagerly. "I've heard of that. It's called a death of a thousand cuts. It's meant to be one of the worst ways to die. Yeah, I reckon we should do that to him. It's what he deserves."

The woman sighed. "Fine, whatever. Why don't you three go have a look what you can find behind the eatery while we keep hold of him. Just be careful in there. There's still a few of those nasty little ones scampering about."

Desmond watched the others run off, leaving just him with these two. He figured that all he had to do now was to find some way of disabling just one of them. The cleaner's entrance was only a few minutes from here. Desmond could lose them in the passageways behind the walls. They'd never find him in there.

"Can I slice him first?" asked Mo. "You know, for old time's sake." His dark eyes focussed on Desmond. "To show this dirty little thief that I'm not an idiot, and I know he's been stealing food for months."

The woman told him to be quiet. "Don't let her speak to you like that," said Desmond. "By the way, I once crapped on your desk. I wiped it everywhere too."

"I'm going to enjoy cutting you up, you vile little man." He drew his index finger along Desmond's forehead. "That's where I'll make the first cut."

"I mean it, shut it, both of you."

Desmond had no intention of being quiet, not now he'd seen what the woman had spotted. "You like to spy on people. I guess that's part of your job, but I watch and notice things too. Like that time when you were rubbing yourself this morning when that woman bent over in the eatery. Bet you even have a camera installed in her office too. In the toilets as well, I bet."

The man clenched his fist and swung his arm back. "One more word," he yelled. "Go on, I dare you!"

Mo obviously hadn't noticed the blood draining from the woman's face or that they now had company. Who'd have thought it would have been so easy to aggravate a security guard? Desmond thought that having a thick skin kinda came with the job. Like a thick hide that comes with that dinosaur currently sneaking up behind Mo. A dinosaur which Desmond had seen before. He wanted to hum a happy little tune. It turned out that somebody *did love* this poor little downtrodden cleaner after all.

The woman had already removed her hands from Desmond's clothing and finally, the penny dropped with Mo. Desmond wasn't sure if it was the sight of his accomplice backing away, Desmond pushing out his tongue, or that perhaps the feathered animal had unintentionally made a noise in its approach. The security guard slowly turned at the exact same time as the dinosaur jumped five feet into the air and performed a vicious roundhouse kick. Its elongated talon sliced through both of Mo's cheeks. It followed this by disembowelling the man before he even fell onto the tiles.

Desmond dropped low when the animal leaped over his head. He stopped grinning at the sight of the dying man's hot blood spreading out from his body and turned to watch the dinosaur jump onto Mrs. Killmore's back. Its jaws fastened around the back of her neck, and within seconds, her shriek was cut short as its curved teeth ripped through skin and muscle.

The rest of Desmond's ill-fated execution squad looked over the sandwich bar counter and, bless their cotton socks, they even had found a couple of knives. Desmond so wanted the dinosaur to run after them too, but it just flipped the woman onto her back and bit out her throat before trotting back over to where Desmond stood. The temptation to pat it on the head was so great. In the end though, he decided against it. He wanted to keep his hand attached to his wrist.

The dinosaur squawked a couple of times, and then ran over to the corridor which led to the toilets. The other three still stared at Desmond from behind the counter. How dumb were they? He gave the buggers a mock bow. "I'm living with the enemy, you bitches," he screamed. Desmond spun around and kicked Mo as hard as he could in the balls before running after the dinosaur. Oh God, he couldn't wait to join up with Zinik-Tow again. He could even forgive his pal for leaving him all alone in that timeship now that he'd sent his pet dinosaur to kill the people wanting to murder this poor janitor. "You need a name, I think. If you don't mind, I'm going to call you after my mother. Yeah, Susan. It's such a fitting name for such a nasty violent bugger like you."

## CHAPTER FIFTEEN

That one was never going to stop begging! She so reminded Gloria of Jessica, her ginger cat. That old thing never knew when to quit either. Still, at least with Jessica, she didn't have to worry about the cat's teeth snapping off the tips of her fingers. "You are such a greedy little monster, Julie," she chided. "For that, you can miss out on your next turn."

She stopped feeding her gathered collection of little brown dinosaurs to watch a larger monster run down and catch a dinosaur with a large frill on its neck. She hadn't seen one of those in here before. It sure did look familiar. Lordy, Gloria so wished David was here with her. That clever young man knew all their names. She remembered just a couple of weeks ago when the store refreshed the stock for the toy fixture. He got so excited when one of the boxes contained a bunch of plastic dinosaurs. He then did something very naughty and ripped open one of the packets. David just smiled at her and said it must have been damaged in transit when she raised the issue.

Gloria tore off a strip of meat and threw it at Jasmine. Unlike Julie, that one hadn't moved off the red plastic chair. She was such a good girl. David had lined up all the little dinosaurs on an upturned box, and then flicked three of them onto the floor. When she had asked why he'd done that, David explained that those crappy Chinese-made toys weren't anatomically correct. He said that a *Stegosaurus*, a *Diplodocus*, and an *Ankylosaurus* never had teeth like a pissing lion. She looked into the mouths of her new friends. Both Julie and Jasmine belonged to the same species, and they certainly had teeth like a pissing lion. Her new friend dwarfed Julie and Jasmine. She had named her *Jane*, and her teeth were even larger. "You lot aren't crappy Chinese made toys, that's for sure!" She giggled when Jane put out her forearm. Gloria clapped in delight. "That is so cute!" She threw Jane a larger piece. "David would know what you were called."

Gloria wiped her bloodied fingers on the side of her uniform and thought back to when all this weirdness started. She knew

David had sneaked off again. The little scamp was terrible for shying away when the store was quiet. Still, he was young though, and back then, she didn't have any care about developing a work ethic either. As long as David didn't pull his trick when there were lots of people in the shop, she'd keep his secret between themselves.

She turned around, watching some more commotion just outside the eatery. That was the mall manager and that security guard who'd helped her the other day. He was such a nice man. Gloria wondered why they had that janitor. She didn't like him at all. The way those creepy eyes stared at you, it fair made her feel dirty inside. Gloria let them to get on with whatever they were up to. It had nothing to do with her.

Gloria hoped both David and Jefferson were all right. She had seen quite a lot of people come and go while she'd been sitting here, opposite the Chinese buffet stall. Gloria had seen quite a lot of people being eaten up as well. She pulled off another strip of meat; this time, she gave it to Julie. Thankfully, none of those eaten people were her fellow work colleagues. Gloria wouldn't know if she'd be able to keep her usual chilled out state if David was dead. He always used to say that she'd make a fortune if she could bottle her placid composure.

Maybe if all those silly people would calm down and maybe stop running about then those dinosaurs wouldn't be eating them. It was like dogs, really. Her mum always told her never to run from a barking dog. Not that dogs ever did bark at her. Gloria always had a way with animals, no matter what species they belonged to.

Both Julie and Jasmine had a long neck, a bit like an ostrich but without beaks attached to their small heads. Their lizard tails and thin, long arms made it clear that they weren't birds. Yet, the new addition turned Gloria's theory right on its head as Jane sported a plumage which belonged on one of those birds of paradise. Unless Jane had ripped the feathers off those birds. "Is that what you did, Jane, you naughty bully?" The dinosaur tilted its head to the side and let out a squeak. It then lowered its body and bobbed its head up and down.

"Okay, I get it, ladies. Stop it with the yapping and hand out more tasty bits." She threw them all some more lumps of meat. "You are such funny onions."

The event beyond the tables took a turn for the worse when another larger dinosaur sneaked out from the toilet areas. It looked very much like Jane but three times the size, and probably twice as mean.

Gloria busied herself with keeping her new friends happy when the blood began to flow. Thankfully, the fun and games only lasted a few minutes. While she threw another treat to Jane, Gloria wondered if it was bad of her to wish the ill-tempered dinosaur had chewed up the nasty janitor as well.

She switched her gaze from that horrid man's departing form to give Julie such a look. "Now, you. Don't start this again, little lady. I thought you'd already learned your lesson. I've only just given you a piece!" She jumped back in her chair when all three leaped onto the table, bent their heads, and hissed at Gloria before jumping down and darting in opposite directions.

"Well, that's charming," she muttered. "Leave me here and alone. See if I care."

"Would you mind if I sat on your table?"

Gloria blinked away the surprise. Where had he come from? Gloria's hearing was much better than most, but she hadn't heard this one at all. Gloria smiled up at this handsome young man. Not that she was going to complain. He might have given *creeping* Jesus a run for his money, but this one sure was prettier.

"Not at all. Just mind the mess. My three previous fair-weather friends don't have the greatest of table manners." She clamped her jaw shut, aware that the sudden presence of this mysterious, pretty thing had caused her to run off at the mouth. Where had this one come from? He certainly didn't look at all bothered about this dinosaur invasion or that the tiles were covered in bloodied chunks of meat.

"I find you fascinating. You do not fit into any of the several social behavioural categories that I have used to define your confusing species." He placed his hands on the table and leaned forward. "Does my presence trouble you?"

"Oh my, you sure know how to charm a girl off her feet," she replied sarcastically. "I'll tell you what. Why don't we start again, this time with an easier sentence? I know. Why don't you tell me your name? I'll go first. I'm Gloria. It's a pleasure to meet you."

It was weird to her how his face seemed to shift. One second he was the spit of that pretty boy advertising Cougar aftershave, who was currently gracing the window of Sandy's store. The next he looked just like her father, back when she saw a little girl. Gloria had to look away before he gave her a headache.

"You wish to know my full name? I am not sure that is appropriate, considering you are just a herd creature." He moved his chair to the side when Gloria's three friends reappeared and danced beside her. "That is something which I did not think possible," he said looking at the three killers.

She pulled off three more strips and threw them into the air. It was nice that the three girls had returned. Also, this new chap didn't look all too bothered about his presence. "I'm happy with which name you give me, honey. Whatever makes you comfortable."

"I am Dailess-Zaid. Destroyer of Cetis Five, devourer of the Sons of Maulis-Bow, and first commander of the Soorlin-Del Quantum Capsule."

"Well that's a bit of a mouthful for little old me. Will you mind if I just call you Dailess-Zaid?" Gloria leaned forward and studied this rather charming young man. He was so out of place in here. In fact, if she wasn't wrong, it might be more out of this world. "So, I take it all this disruption is your doing?"

"Why would you suppose that?"

She shrugged. "I guess your long name does kinda give away your job, honey. There aren't many folk who wash cars or hand out fries who have such a fancy title." The three girls had gone again. Not too far this time, though. They decided that the ex-mall manager's ripped-open throat was a more attractive meal.

"This was my laboratory. I am a cautious individual. More cautious than others of my race. I believed study and experimentation was the desired cause of action in this alien environment. Yet, despite my cautiousness, nothing has gone to plan. My race is doomed to extinction."

He looked up from the table.

"I followed doctrine for first contact. I sealed and subjugated this dwelling's inhabitants. I learned everything I could about your present conditions as well as your extraordinary rise to becoming the top of the food chain. Doctrine is adamant regarding the cataloguing of a new species. Everything from the species genetic assembly to social and historical references. This needs to be complete before we remove you hairless vermin from the surface of the world you stole from us."

Gloria nodded in sympathy. It was nice to see that someone else hadn't been having a great day either. She wanted to tell him that at least he didn't have to worry about the casserole she'd placed in the slow cooker before starting work. By now, it was bound to be burnt to a crisp, unless Mrs. Jackson from number ten had popped round to check on her. No, she decided not to share that with this handsome man. He had enough problems.

"I followed doctrine and yet I failed. Even the annihilation of your species has not gone to plan. My techs did not anticipate the vast amount of genetic diversity within the individual we used to seed the contagion. We do have two more infected, but they escaped before we could displace them to the other continents."

Gloria patted the back of his hand. "Sounds to me like you haven't had the best of days." She slid her cardboard cup across the table; thankfully the three girls hadn't knocked it off the table. "I think you need this more than I do."

He ran a finger around the rim. "A liquid?"

She giggled. "You sure are quick. Yes, it's a lovely cup of tea. A cup of tea makes everything better. That's what my dad always used to say."

"I still don't understand what compelled me to speak to you. Doctrine commands that all lower forms of sentient life insult the Great Deity."

"I wouldn't let a little thing like that worry you too much, love. I've always had a way with animals." She looked him straight in the eye. "And I think you fall into that category, love, because you sure as heck are not human, despite that fancy gadget you're using to mask your proper face."

"After a comment like that, I should strike you down."

"You'd better drink your tea before it gets cold." She lightly squeezed his hand. "Before you do that though, perhaps you had better finish what you started. You'll feel better for it, believe me. Problems are always better when you share them."

He tapped his finger on the table. "This one here, the one you call Jane. She is my ancient ancestor. My species evolved from her. She is a formidable predator. Her intelligence, speed, and cunning is matched with her bloodlust. This animal feasted on the vermin which would eventually give rise to your pitiful species."

Gloria clicked her fingers, and Jane hopped up to her side. She tickled the animal under the snout before she gave it another piece of meat. "Did Jasmine and Julie change too?"

He nodded. "Yes. We were not the first sentient species to develop. Four million years before we became self-aware, the older ones ruled two continents. Their mistake was to allow the creatures we evolved from to continue existing, for once we were able, our race exterminated every last one of them. It took the best minds from our technician caste four centuries to reverse engineer and decode their technology. Once those obstacles were down, our race spread out amongst the stars. We discovered over-intelligent species, and as doctrine demanded, they were crushed utterly."

"And now the shoe is on the other foot, love? For here you are, living amongst the hairless vermin. From what I've guessed, the people beyond the mall are probably dying?"

"Not everyone. Mortality rates appears to be levelling off at sixty per eighty."

"Still, that does leave a lot of people left alive who'll no doubt be rather upset at your failed attempt to cleanse their friends and family." She watched Julie and Jasmine playing hide and seek under the tables. She smiled. It was so nice to see them play. They so reminded her of her two young cats back home. Gloria blinked. Goodness, she hoped they'd be okay. If the people truly were dying in the streets, she doubted her friend would be popping across to check on that casserole, meaning that her little fur babies would be getting very hungry about now. This was a bit of a pickle. "It's likely that the last few of you could end up having the stuffing knocked out of you once you do leave the mall?"

"No. That will never happen. Your primitive weapons are like toys to my shock troops. There is nothing that your soldiers possess which will even scratch their armour of the warrior caste."

"I'm sure a dozen nuclear warheads might give them a bit of a headache, though."

"Even your species are not insane. They would not use that amount of firepower on their own civilians."

She sighed. "So much for you studying our behaviour." Then again, it didn't shock her that much. Some folk who are further up the ladder don't always see the world the same way as the little people. Her boss was just the same. Not Mr. Hussain. He was nice. The man who came around once a month, dressed in that posh suit, with his two attached office monkeys. Now he didn't truly understand the mind of the common people. If he had, the silly man wouldn't suggest a gourmet section and fill it with items over £4, believing the company would only grow by attracting a better class of people.

"Dailess, love. People panic. Folks do not behave in a rational way. They certainly don't when they see their loved ones and strangers dropping like flies. It won't take long for the source to be discovered. Do you not think the other countries won't do anything when they see pictures of your big, hard soldiers prancing about and shooting things with their ray guns? You'll have a hundred nuclear missiles on your heads before you can say *Jiminy Cricket*. I'm sorry, love, but that's just how it is."

The poor man looked just like a feeding goldfish. Gloria guessed that he wasn't expecting the truth. It was just the same when the boss was walking around the shop. He had his monkeys agreeing to his plans of stocking all this lobster and venison, explaining to Mr. Hussain that the common folk would likely be suspicious at first, perhaps even fascinated. In the end though, they'd follow the lead of their betters and snap it up. Poor Mr. Hussain was clearly uncomfortable. He knew the shoppers would have it all right, the stuff would walk out under their coats. That was the hard truth. It's just how it was. Gloria pulled the cap off the cup and took a sip. The tea wasn't quite cold. "Love, you're the one who called us *herd creatures*. Don't they panic at the sight of a predator?"

He nodded. "Then we are truly doomed. I have failed my people."

Jane was now decidedly most upset when Julie and Jasmine came back to her, obviously expecting some more treats. "Stop that, you naughty girl. There's enough for everyone." She gave them all some more meat, nodding and smiling when she saw her handsome chap drinking the tea.

Gloria took his free hand again. "Calm yourself down, dear. It's never as bad as you think. Trust me. I know these things."

"I should be consulting Doctrine on what to do." He sighed. "Why are you even helping me? This is one matter that I do not understand. I have tried to destroy your entire race. You should be wanting to kill me. The animals which are under your spell are quite capable of pulling me apart. You could quite easily order them to do so."

"Is that what Doctrine would be suggesting? As for the people who have died, most of them will have been arseholes anyway."

He jumped up, his chair falling backwards, startling the three meat-eaters. "You dare to insult Doctrine? The word of the Great Deity has enabled our species to be the absolute masters of twenty-five star systems for over two million years. I should not have to listen to the words vomiting from some mammal of low intelligence."

Gloria drained the tea that he had left before pulling off some more meat strips for when her girls came back. She looked up at the furious creature and gave him a smile. "If you've finished, perhaps you'd like to sit back down again, or perhaps you might want to stamp your feet and say that life isn't fair?"

"Do not call me *Dailess, love* again," he muttered.

She allowed him to sit back down before speaking. "I am a mammal, love. I know that, but as for low intelligence, well that depends on what you are comparing me with. Dailess-Zaid, I know that your species evolved in an alternate timeline. One where the asteroid never wiped out the dinosaurs. I know that you are from a rigid society where the idea of sudden change is alien. I believe that is so rigid that even your soldiers and scientists are now close to becoming a sub-species." She shuffled in her chair. "That, is the kicker. As you are all so fabulously xenophobic, the very idea of inter-caste mating churns your stomach."

"You have given me much to think about."

"Fine, just don't take too long about it, love. Even with most of the human race wiped out, the ones remaining will bounce back." She looked up to the ceiling. "I'm guessing that the rest of your friends and your time machine thingy are up there. My advice is take everything that belongs to you, including all your friends, and find somewhere nice and quiet, live a happy life. Believe me, love. If any of your stuff fell into the hands of our men in white coats, it won't take them four hundred years to work out how it all works." She paused. "It was twenty-five star systems you annihilated? Well, here, in this timeframe, those people are not dead. How would they react if they found out about you?"

"That would be suicide. They would target this planet and vapourise it. The humans would not do such a—"

Gloria held up her hand. "We've already been down this road, love."

He stared at the three dinosaurs crouching beside the woman. "Do you wish to go home? Displacing you would be the least I could do for the help you have been."

"Sure, but I can't leave my three girls here."

"Would you not be worried that the predators would not consume your cats?"

"Oh, you know what fur babies are?"

He smiled. "No, I did not. I consulted the ship's index first."

Gloria tickled Jasmine under the chin, and then did the same to Julie when she began to squawk. "You are such a jealous lump." Gloria shook her head. "No, they won't fight. Maybe Jessica will probably get a bit moody, but as long as they don't lie in her bed, she'll soon come round eventually."

He stood. "Do not move from this area. I will be back presently. Wait, before I do go. Tell me, what you are feeding these animals."

"Oh, that's my boss, Mr. Hussain. I found the poor chap lying beside this table with most of his insides missing and no head. I guess he'd must have fallen foul of one of the bigger dinosaurs. Still, it did seem a shame to waste him."

Gloria watched the strange man vanish, taking the corner of the table with him. "That is a neat little trick. I wonder which race you stole that from." She got out of her seat and wandered over to the burger stand to get herself another cup of tea. This saving what remained of the human species was thirsty work.

## CHAPTER SIXTEEN

Out of the group, it appeared that only Sandy and Janine had been able to keep their heads. Even when Sandy had bent down to tie her shoelaces and the hippo-sized soldier pushed the gun's muzzle against her head, she still remained cool as a cucumber. Oh Christ. Her head could have fit inside that sodding barrel!

Janine's death grip was hurting his fingers, but Jefferson dare not say anything in case any of those huge lizard-bird-things took a sudden dislike to his face. The crossbow was still in his other hand. That felt so unreal. The bastards hadn't even bothered snatching it away. It's like they already knew that it posed about as much danger to them as a pissing egg whisk.

One of them had already had a go at David. The one standing next to Janine, currently stuffing its ugly face with some more of that dead dinosaur, lightly tapped his friend on the shoulder a couple of minutes ago. Jefferson guessed that the thing wasn't too happy about David's sobbing. The blow had thrown the poor lad into one of the stone pillars. Even Sandy had winced at the impact.

A couple of sharp jabs with one of those guns encouraged David to get back onto his feet. His friend now leaned against the pillar. He hadn't stopped sobbing. Jefferson didn't think that he was likely to stop anytime soon either.

After all the disruption, the slaughter, and hurt he'd ridden through, David had finally broken with watching Alan die and literally fall apart. He and Alan had been close. Jefferson knew that. Despite the lad's childish behaviour and his apparent disregard for basic social interaction, he had helped Alan through two break-ups. He'd even offered his bedroom when Alan's parents threw him out. Knowing their history made it all the harder to understand why the little bastard had run out on them and put them into this dire position in the first place.

Jefferson wished he'd stop it with the waterworks before the lad got him crying too.

The hippo-sized soldiers were now chirping in that weird bird-like language. Their leader fiddled with a device the size of a tablet, on his thick wrist. Jefferson bit down on his bottom lip when his dam of bottled-up emotions threatened to burst.

A thin, warbling noise erupted from the creature's device. Immediately, every soldier went down on one knee and bowed their heads. Even the ones guarding the group followed suit. Janine smiled at Jefferson before she caught Sandy's eye. What were they up to? Jefferson's silent enquiry went unanswered as the air in front of the leader shimmered and another form appeared.

Jefferson tried to jump back only for Janine to jerk him closer to her. He blinked rapidly, finding it hard to focus on the image. It hurt his eyes. He shut them for a moment and only opened them again when another chirping voice broke the silence. He found himself looking at another weird reptilian bird creature. Although it bore some resemblance to the hippo soldiers, it was built more like a human. From what Sandy and Alan had described, it was too well built to be one of the crane-like creatures they fought in inside that structure.

Jefferson wondered if he was looking at one of the big guys, the ones in charge. The soldiers' behaviour certainly supported that idea. The new creature's rapid chirping was making every soldier shiver. Jefferson so wished he knew what they were saying to each other. Whatever is was, it didn't sound good. That much he was sure about.

Janine let go of his hand and then reached over and dragged David towards them, keeping her gaze fixed on the soldiers. David didn't react to her taking his hand. The lad looked utterly stoned out of his box. His friend's unusual behaviour concerned him more than whatever Janine and Sandy were up to. She had taken Janine's place by taking Jefferson's hand. He tried not to shiver in anxiety at what Sandy had planned.

"Don't do this, Sandy," he hissed. Jefferson tensed up when one of the soldiers moved its head. "Please, they'll kill us all."

The girl put her heel on his toe. "Stop fretting, you," she whispered, while grinning.

She raised her other arm. He now saw she had something held in her hand. It looked like a gun, a gun which looked just like the ones clipped to the belts of the hippo soldiers. Oh fuck! Sandy hadn't been tying her lace after all! Jefferson wasn't the only one to notice Sandy moving. The blue hologram chirped out an incomprehensible noise as well. The leader spun around at the exact moment that Sandy fired.

The air filled with the stench of ozone and burning meat as the leader's whole body just deflated. His armour clattered to the floor. All that remained of the creature's flesh were a few blackened toes. The other soldiers jumped to their feet and screamed in unison. They were acting like crazed chickens at the sight of a fox.

Janine and David had already started running. Sandy dragged Jefferson away from the panicking soldiers. It took him a second for his dazed mind to catch up with what had just happened. He shook away the malaise and ordered his legs to function properly. Jefferson found his feet and raced after the other two, still keeping a tight grip of Sandy's hand. Amazingly, she was laughing. If it wasn't for having to leave Alan behind, he probably would have joined in.

David had woken up enough to inform Janine that the two huge dinosaurs inside the pet shop were *Triceratops*. He seemed to be having difficulty in trying to figure out how they had gotten inside the shop without breaking the glass as they sure as hell hadn't walked through the door.

Janine glanced over her shoulder. She winked at Sandy, and then blew Jefferson a kiss. He couldn't help but to smile back. They had gotten away. He didn't know how, but they had. Janine stopped by the doors which led to the lower level. She peered through the glass before nodding.

Jefferson stopped when he reached his friends and turned around. He heard their screams, but he couldn't see the soldiers. He got the feeling that they hadn't even noticed that their prisoners had gone. Janine's arms snaked around his waist. She kissed the back of his neck.

"We're still alive!" she said.

"They're all in deep shock," said David. The lad sighed heavily. He then looked straight at Jefferson. "I know how that feels. Dude. I'm really sorry for running out on you." He turned to Sandy. "I guess I panicked. Shit, I'm such a shit."

Sandy wrapped her arm around him and kissed the tip of his nose. "No, you're just *you*." She gingerly handed the creature's device over to Jefferson. "I think you had better take charge of this. It's too scary for me."

"Listen to you, girl. I don't think you even know the meaning of the word." Jefferson held the gun tightly, surprised at its lightness. It looked and felt exactly like the dart guns they sold in Alan's shop.

"David. What do you mean that they're all in shock?"

"It's quite simple, Sandy. They operate as a single unit, with the squad commander acting like the nexus for each individual. I believe that it isn't just training that has made them so efficient. It's breeding too. They are genetically predisposed to behave as they did."

"Well, that's cleared that up," replied Sandy. "Now how about repeating that in English?"

"Think of them as a living organism, and you have just melted the brain and the heart."

"Time to go?"

Jefferson turned around in Janine's embrace. "I think so." He kissed her soft lips. "Yeah, time to go. I mean, it's not like there's anything left that can stop us now, is there?"

Sandy and David pushed through the doors and made their way down the stairs. Jefferson untangled himself from Janine, grabbed her hand and then ran down the stairs, needing to get to the bottom before Sandy. They might have left the soldiers on the next floor but they sure as hell weren't in the clear just yet. He couldn't work out if Sandy was fearless or just plain stupid.

He grabbed her arm just before they reached the doors.

"Wait on, how did you know that those soldiers wouldn't melt us back in the department store? I mean, I thought we were all dead."

She looked over at Janine before she unfolded her sleeve. "Take a look at this."

An irregular-shaped patch of red skin ruined Sandy's otherwise perfect tan. She gently pressed her forefinger against the blemish, and Jefferson winced as her fingernail broke through the softened skin. She pulled the finger away then looked up and Jefferson. "It's happening to me as well," she uttered. "Only whatever it is they injected inside me is acting a lot slower than it did with Alan." She folded the sleeve over the blemish. "I don't think that either Alan or I are infectious. Although I think that was what they intended. That's why we were spared, Jefferson. We were supposed to spread this to everybody else." She shrugged. "I guess they fucked up somewhere along the line."

"Oh no." Jefferson took hold of her hands. "There must be something we can do to stop it from spreading!"

Fat tears rolled down Sandy's cheeks. "I hope so," she said quietly. "I don't want to go the same way as Alan."

Janine opened the doors and held them open as they walked through. "Nothing has changed. We still need to get out of this damned place and find a doctor. Until then, Sandy, I suggest that you try to stop thinking about your arm and focus on trying to stay alive." She pointed over at the pretzel stand. "For example. How the how do we get past that thing?"

"Oh my God!" uttered David. "That's a Tyrannosaur! A real, proper T-rex. Look at the size of the thing, just look at it! My God!"

He spun around to stare at Jefferson. His face shone as bright as a torch. He couldn't believe the change in the lad. It wasn't that long since David looked ready to top himself. Is that all it took to bring the lad out of his slump? He chided himself for acting like an arse again. It wasn't David's fault that his passion made him seem so heartless on the surface.

"I wonder what it's doing?"

"Waiting to be served," replied Sandy. "Look, does it matter? Jefferson, melt the bastard. We haven't got time to go around it."

The huge animal lowered its head until it was level with the counter. The Tyrannosaur's wet nostrils quivered. Could it smell them? Jefferson slowly put his hand on the door behind him. Even with this *out of this world* weapon, he still didn't feel safe. At the first sign of it about to charge, he intended to push his friends through into the stairwell and run like hell.

The sheer size and power of this animal turned Jefferson's blood into ice-slush.

"She right," hissed Janine. "We can't go around it." It suddenly opened its canyon jaws and roared. The noise was like standing directly under a landing jumbo jet. Sandy clamped her hands over her ears. The sleeve fell away from her arm, exposing the infected skin. Jefferson was sure the redness had spread further down her arm. What the hell was he hesitating for? He was wasting time while another one of his friends was dying right in front of his eyes!

Jefferson raised his hand, aimed at the dinosaur's head, and pressed what looked like a trigger. Nothing happened.

The tyrannosaur roared again, and this time, it didn't look like it was going to stay beside that pretzel stall.

"I don't know what to do with this thing!"

Sandy grabbed Jefferson's arm and snatched the weapon out of his hand. The huge beast lumbered towards them, still roaring. The stench of its foul breath now filled the air. The noise even shook Jefferson's bones. He backed away, getting ready to pull his friends into the stairwell, when Sandy finally got it to fire again.

A hot stream of energy slammed into the creature's head. The shot liquefied skin and bone.

"Oh my God!" moaned David. He ran over to a litterbin and dropped to his knees.

Jefferson grabbed the two women and jerked them over to the doors when the headless body tilted over before crashing into the pretzel stand. Splintered pieces of bright orange painted wood flew out in every direction.

David came back over to the group. He wiped his mouth with the back of his hand. "Sorry about that," he muttered. The lad turned around, his head facing the dead dinosaur. "Weird, I thought they would be bigger."

"You two okay?" Jefferson brushed a few flecks of orange paint from Janine's top, noting that Sandy had already fastened up her sleeve. He so didn't want to be the realist in this, but he doubted that there would be any medical expert on this planet who would be able to save his friend. Not after witnessing what their weapons could do. "Sandy, how the hell did you make it fire?"

She shrugged. "I did exactly what you did, Jefferson." She turned it around in her hand. "It feels lighter now, also, have you noticed the colouring? I'm sure the colours were deeper. God, listen to me banging on again." She pushed passed them and slammed a hand on David's shoulder. "Come on, you. Stop staring at it. We need to get out of here. Once you have seen one Tyrannosaur, I guess you've seen them all."

David shook his head. "We're not going anywhere," he cried, his shaking hand pointing towards exactly where they all needed to go.

Jefferson rushed up to Sandy and David. His jaw dropped at the sight of dozens of two-legged dinosaurs all running towards where they stood. "The meat! They must be after the meat." He fumbled his last bolt into the groove. "Come on, move back, all of you. We've gone through this before. As long as we don't disturb them."

His friend stumbled past him. "Not this time!" he shouted. David took hold of his hand. "We need to get out of here. They're not after food, the bastards are running away from something. Just look at them, they're terrified!"

Jefferson jumped to the side when three small brown dinosaurs, just like the ones that were attacking David in the eatery, ran past them. He looked back over at the doors, thinking that maybe David was right. None of them were taking a slightest bit of interest in the dead Tyrannosaur. Jefferson almost freaked when he saw another face on the other side of that door staring right back at him. One of the soldiers had followed them. "We need to get out of here!"

None of the others had heard a word he said. Jefferson slowly turned his head and screamed at the sight of another two Tyrannosaurs walking around the corner of the concourse. Only these were twice the size of the one that Sandy had killed. He dropped the crossbow, took hold of Sandy, and joined the panicking flow of the smaller animals. David had already reached the eatery, and he pulled him onto a table when Jefferson reached him. They both grabbed the hands of the girls and lifted them out of the swarm.

"We need to hide!" David ran down the middle of the eatery, followed by the others.

Jefferson heard the sound of that energy beam firing, followed by an inhuman scream. He didn't think that scream belonged to any of those dinosaurs. He heard himself whimpering while both

Sandy and Janine helped him to scramble over the counter of the sandwich shop. What were they going to do now?

## CHAPTER SEVENTEEN

This feathered fuckwit wasn't exactly the best conversationalist. Not that Desmond was all that bothered. He rather enjoyed the silence after his fellow workmates had betrayed this poor janitor. Yeah well, Susan here sure fixed their wagons, that's for damned sure! It took him a full two minutes to stop grinning after watching Susan rip those two losers apart. They sure weren't going to insult Desmond anymore.

They were now close to the chamber, to where he was supposed to be meeting up with Zinik-Tow. It seemed like a weird choice of meeting place. Wouldn't it have been better to meet his pal in a cafe or something? Now that it looked like he was out of danger, Desmond's stomach reminded him to put something in there. To think that not too long ago, he had some rather nice chicken in his hands.

Susan stopped besides a large bundle of crumpled clothing. It was only when she dipped her head and tore out a strip of muscle when Desmond discovered it wasn't just fabric lying on the concrete floor. Pieces of the owner still remained inside.

He crouched beside the raptor who'd now pushed her muzzle deep inside the mess, intending to examine the clothing. The dinosaur lifted her head and snapped at him, her teeth just missing her fingers by millimetres.

"Will you stop it off, you annoying pain in the arse?" he yelled. "I don't want to steal your stinking dinner."

The dinosaur growled before lunging at Desmond. The top of her head smacked into his chest, sending the janitor flying backwards. "Fine then, I'll stay here, feeling the water soak my arse while you fill your guts. See if I care!"

Desmond was beginning to really dislike Susan. He slowly got to his feet, listening to her growling becoming louder. He squinted, while staring hard at the bits of clothing that weren't soaked in blood. He then turned his frown upside down when it dawned on him who used to wear those clothes. Desmond was looking at what remained of the loathsome individual who ran the pet shop on the top level. "Oh what a shame," he said, grinning. "I hope your demise was as painful as it was slow."

He edged his way past the feeding animal, idly wondering why those mall employees hadn't targeted him instead of the pet shop owner. Everybody knew he was up to no good. Yet, they all turned a blind eye to his dodgy dealings. Because this poor janitor just happened to be in the right place at the right time, he was the bad one. They vilified him, that's what they did. Yeah, well... He showed them.

Desmond reached the hatchway. He hoisted himself up and began to crawl through the passageway, so hoping that Susan wasn't a fast eater. The last thing he needed right now was to feel her needle sharp teeth sinking into his buttock cheeks. He quickened his pace at that unpleasant thought.

He dropped into the chamber and found himself sharing the space with nothing but a collection of shattered bones. There was no sign of his new pal. "What the hell is this?" Desmond walked around the perimeter of the chamber, looking in every pipe. He reached the last one the pipes which he saw Susan walking through in what felt like an age ago, and held onto the edge while gaping in utter confusion at the collection of alien-like objects filling the space. Equipment didn't fill all the area. In the middle of the mess, Desmond saw Zinik-Tow furiously labouring over an object which looked very similar to a very small pneumatic drill. If the said object had been dipped into a bath of thick yellow jelly.

"What the frig is that?"

The creature looked up from his work and attempted to smile. "It is good to find that my ancient ancestor was successful in locating you. This is very satisfying news as I need you right now, Desmond." Zinik-Tow stood and leapt along the interior of the pipe, reaching Desmond in moments.

There was something about the way he was looking at this poor janitor that made him feel very uneasy. Especially the way he held that device in both his clawed hands. "Wait, what's that supposed to be?" He stepped back when the creature jumped out of the pipe and landed directly in front of him.

"I am so going to enjoy this," he hissed, raising the device.

Desmond whimpered and ran back to the hatch, only to find Susan coming through it. "Oh god, no. Please don't eat me. I don't want to die down here!"

Zinik-Tow wrapped his claws around the janitor's throat and pulled him back onto his feet. He spun Desmond around and used his own body to hold the shaking man against the wall. "I do envy you," he said before lightly pressing the flattened edge of the device under Desmond's chin. "Give him my regards," he said before he pushed the device into his flesh.

Desmond couldn't even scream before darkness filled his entire world.

*\*\*\**

It felt like somebody had replaced his blood with thick syrup. Desmond saw a flash of intense green light before his body crashed into what felt like a carpet made from potato waffles. He counted to five before daring to open his eyes. He ran his fingers over the grid-like floor while looking around where he'd landed. He sure wasn't in that chamber anymore.

He waited for a moment longer before picking himself up off the floor. Desmond didn't have a clue where he was, nor did he care right now. All that mattered was that he was alone, and this poor janitor believed that this state was better for all concerned. Desmond was so getting fed up with people, dinosaurs, and feathered fuckwits either trying to kill him or tear the flesh his bones.

This wasn't any part of the shopping centre, that much he did know. He was in a curved walkway the width of two cars. The walls were covered in the same waffle pattern as the floor, unlike the floor, the walls were a sickly dark green. The colour was bloody vile. He walked across the outer wall, deciding that whoever had done the decorating had probably bought a van full of the pea-coloured paint at a discount.

He placed his hand against the surface and cried out as the texture flattened out to form a smooth rectangle the height of him and twice as wide. Desmond then stumbled back when the colour vanished, and in its place, he found himself looking down at his home planet. At least, it looked like Earth. Only, the last time he looked, it didn't have two moons, and since when did they have spaceships? Not just one either. The region of space between him and the planet was busier than the dual carriageway outside his house at rush hour. It was around this time when Desmond fully came to realise that he was actually standing inside some kind of space station. "Bloody heck, this is some weird shit going on here!" Desmond backed away from the window, silently wishing the waffle pattern would come back. The view was making him a little sick.

Something told him that he was no longer home. He sighed, like that wasn't obvious already. He shook his head and turned away from the view, deciding that the window wasn't going to disappear after all. The question now was how the bloody hell was he going to get home? Desmond strolled along the curved corridor, staying in the middle, just in case his wandering hands just happened to touch something else. Knowing the shitty luck he'd been having today, his fingers would find a hidden lever that would open a trapdoor under his feet and flush his body out into space.

Then again, did he really want to go back home? "Yeah, I do," he muttered, rubbing his stomach. The walls might look like waffles, but Desmond doubted they'd be edible. He stopped walking when he found he was approaching that big window cut into the waffle wall. He had just walked in a circle. "Hello?" he shouted. "Is there anybody home?"

He stopped by the window again. He watched the spaceships traverse from the two moons, while listening to a rhythmic thud which he felt through the soles of his feet. He found it oddly comforting. Especially as it was the only noise he could hear. Desmond had always preferred the quiet over the mind-draining rasping coming from the gobs of other people.

"Yeah, I do like the quiet."

"Then you will be quite at home here, my young visitor."

Desmond spun around and found a creature which looked very similar to Zinik-Tow staring back at him. "Please don't eat me!" he screamed. Desmond ignored his earlier advice and pressed his whole body against the wall, not caring if he did find his body floating through cold space. Anything would be better than being eaten alive.

"You are a frightful animal. Is the rest of your species like you? If this is the case, then both of our races are destined for extinction." The creature sighed before turning around and walking towards the inner wall. "That would be such a shame. After all the work I have put into this as well." The creature turned its head. "Come along, there is much to discuss and so little time." It pressed one clawed hand against the wall and stood back as a door-shaped section smoothed out before sliding up.

Desmond blinked. Watching the creature stand on the threshold, it put its hands on its hips and sighed again. He decided that it wasn't going to feast on this poor janitor after all. He stood, brushed himself down and walked over to it. Desmond compared this one to Zinik-Tow. Oh, they were clearly the same species, that's for sure. Yet this one appeared to be much older. Not only in its mannerisms either. It kinda reminded him of some old cockerel, long past its invite with the farmer's axe.

He followed it through the door, happy to find smooth grey walls had replaced those disgusting green waffle walls. He saw a line of green letterbox-sized panels at head height. Green writing, at least he assumed it was that, covered each panel. He moved a little closer to the one in front of him wondering what it could say. Desmond did think of asking the creature what it said, but in the end, he backed out. His mind was too busy wondering what the feathered fuckwit tasted like to care about a bunch of stupid signs.

If the push came to the shove, Desmond reckoned that he'd be able to get one over on this old feathered fuckwit. His only problem would be finding a pot large enough to stuff the carcass inside. Oh, and an oven.

"Have I been teleported here or something?"

The creature tutted. "Do not be ridiculous. Displacement field technology can't move you into an extinct timeline. You haven't travelled anywhere, Desmond. Your sleeping form is still where it fell a few moments ago. Now, please, follow me and do be quiet. I am not used to company, especially a lower lifeform which should be in a exhibit." He turned. "Therein lies the paradox which, in your vermin-like way just vomited up." It tapped its claws along the surface of the wall. Another rectangular panel slid away.

Desmond stared in fascination at what, at first glance, looked just like a Hollywood alien. It was suspended in a clear fluid. Several pipes fed out from under its light blue rippled flesh and vanished into a pulsating globe by its three webbed feet.

"You have got to be shitting me," he gasped. Desmond tapped his finger on the glass. "That's an alien! An honest to God proper frigging alien!"

"They called themselves, the Holophours. They were the first exo-planet race which my ancient ancestors annihilated over twelve million years ago. We never called them by their name. To the ones who caused their extinction, they were simply titled 'one' as in *designation one*."

"Wait, is this thing still alive?"

"I see you are most concerned about the destruction of over fourteen billion innocent lives, mammal. I had hope that Zinik-Tow would have chosen a lifeform that at least had some type of empathy built into its basic behaviour." It looked down at its lower arm, plucked out a piece of yellow fluffy down, and watched it as the feather floated to the floor. "Yes, she is still alive. Ironically, it is their technology which keeps all of our exhibits in their state of suspended animation."

"So you have more aliens here? Oh, let me see another one." Desmond hadn't been this excited in years. He used to love watching all those black and white alien invasion movies back when he was a kid. Desmond never actually thought he'd see one. He pried his eyes away from it. "What is this place?"

"The closest analogy which you would understand is that this is a museum. Only you are the first visitor since this structure was towed into this spot. This makes me the curator, the last one from a line that goes back millions of years. My name, for what it is worth, is *Maulis-Bow*."

"Wait, hang on. I know that name. The other feathered fuckwit keeps banging on that you're some kind of God or something." Desmond turned back to the exhibit and ran his fingers along the outer shell. "You sure have a cool job. You have any more I can look at?"

Maulis-Bow nodded. "I have often wondered how different our history would have been if our ancient ancestors had made first contact with another less advanced race than the Holophours. It is likely that the other civilizations would have formed an alliance and wiped out our species before we could do the same to them. You see, Desmond. It took us over twelve thousand years for our early starcraft to cross the vast gulf of space to reach the Holophours' home planet. The devices we sent were not very technologically advanced. Yet, even those primitive ships were not designed by us. Like everything else we have, Desmond, it had belonged to someone else. In this case, the ships were the last product made from the species who once lived with us on our homeworld."

Desmond tried not to yawn.

"Yes, twelve thousand years we waited. It took that alien civilization just two months to make the same distance. They say the Holophours sent thousands of ships, enough to make the sky over capital city go black. It must have been an incredible sight." Maulis-Bow sighed heavily. "The aliens smiled down at us. They wanted to be our friends. In return, we ate them. Our ancestors did not kill them all, not this time. A selected few were kept alive so they could show us how to operate their advanced technology."

Maulis-Bow's claw danced across the panel and dozens more door-shaped compartments opened above and below the other panels. He tapped out another pattern, and the full wall changed to reveal hundreds more compartments. Desmond tilted his head back and counted another sixteen levels, each one holding an alien creature. "There are so many of them!" He ran to the next clear case and pressed his hands and nose flat against the material, utterly transfixed at the creature just inches from his face.

"I call this the Annals of Shame. This selection is all that remains of the three hundred and fourteen species which we have discovered while slowly expanding along the outer spiral arm of this galaxy. In the thirty-four millions years after we acquired the technology to move between the stars in a short time, my species have butchered countless billions of intelligent, beautiful creatures. All because, apparently, their existence insults The Great Deity."

"After all that time, I'm not surprised that you haven't conquered the whole universe by now." Desmond tapped his finger on the glass-like material, so wishing she would open her eyes. Desmond had never seen anyone or anything so beautiful.

This alien's physique closely matched the classic female form but with wider hips, and a chest which would put a porn actress to shame. To complete this picture of Desmond's ideal woman, her silky straw-coloured hair reached almost to her knees. If it wasn't for the fine black- and white-striped fur covering every inch of her boy, she could quite easily pass for any other shopper, as long as she didn't stray into any well lit areas.

Maybe he could shave her? That would be most pleasurable if the old fuckwit would let him bathe this delectable creature in hot soapy water for a few hours. Desmond turned around getting ready to ask the question, only to find him standing right behind him.

"That is designation twenty-one. We never found out what they called themselves. This vile animal is all that is left of their world. Unlike the others we conquered, this species was more violent than we were." He placed his paw on Desmond's shoulder. "Now, turn around, and witness its true form."

Desmond did as he was bid and turned to find a huge black- and white-striped slug-type animal stuck in the transparent material. The image of his dream woman were in pieces. He wanted to sob for her loss. How dare this feathered fuckwit do this to that poor woman. Desmond so wanted to smash its dirty little face in.

The curator pulled him away from the display, and all the aggression seeped out of his bones. He blinked and shook his head, trying to disperse the horrible sensation of supping twelve cans of strong lager. "Okay, that was weird." The creature in the tank, the slug-thing woman now looked very much like a cross between a black and white tapeworm and a funnel.

"Designation twenty-one. This was the first creature we encountered who were able to inflict massive losses upon our troops. You saw how it reacted to you. That thing has been in that booth for millions of years and yet it still lives. They were the apex predator on their world. To them, we were the prey. It was a most disconcerting situation. After two months of these things slaughtering our soldiers, we destroyed their world with Mass Drivers."

Desmond nodded, still feeling shaky, and moved to the next display cabinet with a little more caution. "Okay, I get it. I really do, Maulis-Bow. You've been feeling a bit shit cos all your mates and their great grandaddies are all a bunch of psychopaths. So why should it matter now? I mean, all these aliens are alive again, cos your pal fucked up back in the past."

The curator grinned and nodded. "Indeed. My plans were quite successful." He joined Desmond beside the display case. "This one is designation twenty-nine. They were a peaceful race, like most of the advanced cultures were. Yet, our techs discovered that in their ancient past, these creatures performed genocide on the two co-existing sentient races who once lived on their world. For the first time in our history, we found a species who acted as we did but somehow were able to quell their, as you say, *psychopathic behaviour*."

If it wasn't for the constant grinding coming from his guts, urging Desmond to fill it with food, he believed this place would be a constant source of wonder to behold for days, if not weeks. Even if he had a backpack full of tuna sandwiches, he suspected the backpack would still be full for when he returned to the chamber. His time here was coming to an end. This place no longer felt real anymore, like he was existing in somebody's freaky dream. Which, he suspected, was pretty much what this was.

"They were able to alter their minds and bodies, to splice their species with genetic strands from preserved specimens from their long-dead sister species." His claws danced across the panel and all the display cases closed, returning the wall to its dull uniform grey colour.

"Our time here is running out, so I will have to cut short our tour. It is such a shame, I do miss the company and the exhibits are not great conversationalists. True to be told, neither are you, Desmond, but you are able to respond, if only with simple sentences. It was the discovery of designation twenty-one which showed a select few of our species an alternate way of existence."

Desmond nodded. "You mean not jumping on the heads of every life form you encounter? Okay, so, well done, old guy.

You've done it. All these aliens are now free to frolic in their alien fields, eat their alien food, and it's all happy ever after. Great. So why bother telling all this to some poor janitor?"

The curator wrapped his hands tightly around Desmond's arms. "I think you miss the point. Not that this shocks me. It is quite simple. The Sauron race will live on, only with a few minor alterations. I have made sure of that. We will be like designation twenty-one."

"Wait, Zinik-Tow has this dumb idea about turning himself back into a dinosaur, or some bollocks."

"That is because I did not tell my followers the full story. None of them were ready for the truth. I implicated that we sought out a simpler life, to live like our ancient ancestors. To hunt and to kill our prey. Our species never did this. We were a carrion creature, Desmond. Stealing other kills is a lot easier than the running the risk of killing your own animal. We carried this trait all the way through our lineage."

"Right, you steal other folk's stuff, and then murder them all. Yeah, I can see how this might piss off a few people."

"We murdered our last intelligent species ten years ago. Our technician caste discovered they had cracked the secret of time travel. Zinik-Tow believed that he was on a holy quest for the Great Deity, to destroy the only quantum capsule in existence. I told him he would be restarting our species in our distant past. To fulfil the destiny of the *Sons of Maulis-Bow*."

"He's going to be proper annoyed when he finds out the truth."

The curator shook his head. "No, I think not. He will still fulfil the destiny of the Sons of Maulis-Bow, only with altered parameters. Now, it is time for you to return, Desmond. Your future awaits."

Desmond grinned. "Oh yeah. The making babies part. Yeah, I'm going to enjoy that."

"I am glad you are joyous. You see, it is you who will be restarting our species. You are designation twenty-one."

"Wait, what are you talking about?"

"I have altered your base-line genetic structure, Desmond. You will be the father of a new species. A melding of Human and Sauron. A new hope for this galaxy is now within your cells. In time, I see an alliance of species from all the star systems that the old race once annihilated. The melded species will still rule this galaxy without resorting to violence."

The curator turned Desmond around and led him out of the room and back onto the curved corridor. He took him to the window, which showed thousands of spaceships traversing between the worlds. "It will take thousands of years for our home to resemble the scene you see. It will happen, and this time, it will be without spilling the blood of billions of innocent lives."

The space station, the view outside, and the curator started to fade before Desmond had the chance to asked him exactly what any of that meant, and to tell the idiot that the other clown in that timeship was still alive and kicking and had already started a pissing war against the human race.

## CHAPTER EIGHTEEN

The rough weave between Jefferson's thumb and finger gave him a smidgen of scant reassurance that he really wasn't dreaming anymore. His heart-wrenching shriek had been the catalyst to wrench him out of the terrible certainty of watching those two Tyrannosaurs tear him in two. Even now, with the comforting sounds of his friends' murmurs massaging his ears, Jefferson could still feel the tiles shake as the pair of them lunged towards his trembling body.

He choked back a harsh sob.

"Hush now," said Janine. She crouched beside him and pulled his head against her chest. "It was only a dream."

"How the hell could I could I have fallen asleep, Janine? I feel so stupid. No, I feel irresponsible. It's almost as if I wanted to get everybody killed."

Janine took hold of his chin. "Don't you make me slap you again. I'd much rather kiss those lips. If you keep it up with this pity party, I swear, I'll knock you into next week."

Jefferson shrugged. "Go ahead. It's probably the only way that I'll be able to live past today."

"Look, you slept because you were exhausted, both physically and mentally. Also because for the first time since this madness began, we are all safe."

She helped him onto his feet. Jefferson saw three strangers sat apart from Sandy and David. He also noticed the small group they had bumped into in that restaurant. It pleased him to find they hadn't succumbed to any of the dangers in this mall from hell, but it did sadden him that the group hadn't found a way out of here. It didn't bode well for them at all.

"Tell me what you can hear."

Why was she even asking him this? Then it dawned on him that the music had stopped. He turned his head over to the direction of the counter. The air conditioning wasn't on either. "The power's off. I thought it was a bit dark in here." What was it like in the eatery and in the main area? Oh no, they won't be able to see anything. "We'll have to get some torches!" he gasped. Jefferson remembered that he'd lost the crossbow. They were so dead!

"Will you stop shaking and tell me what you can hear?"

"Apart from our voices, Janine, I can't hear anything."

"Exactly! They've all gone, Jefferson. The dinosaurs aren't on this level anymore."

It took a moment for this news to sink in, and when it did, Jefferson wasn't sure if he should believe it. After all, it's not like they could all vanish into thin air. "Did they find a way out of here? What about going upstairs or out into the carpark, maybe they've all killed each over."

"Slow those horses, cowboy. We've all been through this. Here, drink this, sweetheart." She passed him a cardboard cup. "You need rehydrating."

"What is it?"

"Stop being so suspicious." Janine grinned. "I think you're going to like it."

He took the offered cup and took a sip. He looked in amazement before guzzling it down. Jefferson thought it would be something she'd gotten from this store. "Where did you get the coconut water from? Wait, no, I'm not sure I want to know. Was it David who told you I loved this stuff?"

She linked arms and took him over to David and Sandy. Now that his senses were almost back to full strength, Jefferson felt some kind of atmosphere in the back of this store, and it was all aimed at Sandy. He stopped in front of the girl.

"You okay?"

She slowly nodded. "I've had better days. Still, at least none of me had dropped off yet."

Sandy sounded exhausted. Jefferson gave her a tight hug, partly because he was still glad she was here, and partly to shame the others. He'd already guessed that the new arrivals must have heard about what had happened to them on the upper level, including Sandy and Alan's escaped from that ship of theirs.

David passed him an energy bar. "Here, I saved one for you. I guess you've heard about the mystery of the missing dinosaurs."

Jefferson nodded.

"Well, me and Janine had a bit of a scout about ten minutes ago, and I reckon we can easily make it to the furniture shop. Thing is, there's only you who's been able to get through and—"

"And we're going to need you to show us how you did it."

He hadn't noticed Janine's friend had walked up behind him. "Hello again, Lindsey. It's good to see you again." It disturbed Jefferson a little to see the woman's eyes giving Sandy the occasional glance, and when his friend moved a little closer to David, Lindsey took a slight step back.

"What happened to you and your little group, Lindsey? I don't want to be funny, but I was kinda hoping not to see you in here again."

The woman's face clouded over. She momentarily lost her aura of calmness. "Jesus, I thought we'd had it bad before. When those bird-things took control of our minds..." Lindsey grabbed Jefferson's hand. "To be honest with you. I'm not sure I can repeat what happened to us while trying to get out. We were stupid not to follow your advice. See, Kevin wasn't too happy about going downstairs, so we pursued our original objective to get to the carpark. Oh God, if you hadn't given that sword to Kevin, none of us would be here right now. They were all in that dark corridor when they..."

Janine let go of Jefferson and hugged her friend. "Stop thinking about it. They've all gone now. Come on, let's see you." She turned and smiled at Jefferson. "Are you okay to move?"

He looked into his empty cup, and then placed it on a table. "Oh God yeah!"

She wiped Lindsey's face. "There, that's better. We can't have your friends seeing you like that, honey. You're their rock, remember. Jefferson, grab the others, we'll meet you out front."

He nodded and watched her take Lindsey over to Kevin and Margaret. Kevin had fashioned a scabbard from what looked like a couple of belts and half a shoe. He'd also removed his shirt, tied a red bandana around his forehead, and painted a few thick black lines down his cheeks. If it wasn't from Lindsey's very brief recant of what happened in that corridor and Jefferson's imagination filling in the blanks, he might have laughed at his ridiculous-looking man. Then again, perhaps not. Jefferson didn't think he'd be able to find any joyous emotion in his tired frame for a long time. He turned his attention to the three others who'd tagged along, wondering about their story. Jefferson felt no inclination to go over and introduce himself. He had no inclination to do anything but to get the fuck out of here.

"How long have I been out, David?"

Both Sandy and David had joined him by the counter of the sandwich shop. He leaned over and scanned the area, still expecting to see a bunch of little dinosaurs to start galloping toward him. Jefferson was right about needing some light. Everything was draped in shadow, yet it wasn't totally pitch black. The yellow emergency lights were still working.

"Not long. Probably about an hour tops." David took Sandy's hand. "I know this is going to sound mega weird, but I so *miss all the dinosaurs.*" He gave Sandy a sad smile. "Okay, maybe that's a bit of an exaggeration."

Were they together now? He couldn't even find strength to ask or to be all that surprised at this new development. Jefferson waited for the others to catch up before he climbed onto the counter and jumped down on the other side. He walked between the tables, heading towards the main concourse, keeping his ears open and his eyes alert for anything that might pose a danger.

He knew there were two men carrying swords behind him and yet Jefferson was still in the lead? Since when did he become the leader of this unlikely collection of survivors? If any of the Tyrannosaurs were still around, how was he going to protect everyone? Then again, he doubted the swords would be of much use either. They might as well be armed with frigging cutlery.

Jefferson stopped when he reached the last table; he found his legs totally refused to respond to his commands. What if those two hellish creatures were still in here? He grabbed the edge of the table, suddenly feeling very faint. They couldn't have gone anywhere else. Unlike all the other dinosaurs, they were far too big to go through any door. He couldn't go out there. Jefferson's nightmare would come true if he moved. It was that simple.

"It is safe, you know, honey."

He jumped. So much for keeping his ears on high alert. Jefferson hadn't heard Janine until she was right on top of him.

"No, we're not," he whispered back. It took a lot of effort not to turn around and push through all these strangers and go hide himself in a box. "Those two Tyrannosaurs are still out there. They're too big to go anywhere else."

She shook her head. "Believe me, they're not. We've checked." She pointed over at the grocery store, next to Alan's toy shop. "That's where I got you the coconut water. Nothing tried to bite me in the arse. There's nothing out there." She then turned around and whispered something.

Of all the things to be terrified of, Jefferson guessed that huge Tyrannosaurs weren't a bad thing. It's not like it was spiders or mice or, in Gloria's case, pen tops. Christ, he so hoped she was okay. Jefferson looked over his shoulder and frowned when he noticed a single cup sitting on the table where she always used to sit. Jefferson was sure that wasn't there when he rescued David from the seal thigh dinosaurs. It would be just like his workmate to go have a cup of tea when there were loads of carnivorous dinosaurs running around. She wouldn't have batted an eyelid. That woman would walk through a tropical storm and still be humming some melodious tune. It made him wonder just how many others were still alive in the mall, all hiding away, watching from the safety of their refuge, just waiting for someone like him to show that it was safe to come out now.

"We're all waiting on you, Jeffdude."

Sandy stood by him, grinning. It felt so weird to hear someone else call him that name. "Sorry, I was just waiting for everybody to catch up."

"Sure, I can buy that." She gently tapped the gun she'd picked up outside the department store. "You know something? I don't think this device really belonged to those soldiers." She chuckled. "Okay, that's what David thinks. He says that it's biotech. He also said that they probably stole it from some other species."

"So?"

"Don't you get it? This means that this is alien. It's a proper alien gun. How cool is that?" Sandy stroked its side. "It wouldn't fire for you, Jefferson, because it didn't recognise your hand. It looks a lot better now, don't you think?"

He just looked at her, unsure of why she was telling him all this.

"It does look a lot better now. The colour's come back to it. Which is good." Sandy then linked arms and pulled onto the concourse. "Oh, and if there are any dinosaurs still here, I'll just melt their heads, like I did with the last one."

"I'd love to know what Janine just said to you," he muttered. Jefferson had to admit, he didn't feel so scared with her by his side, or maybe it was more the case that she carried possibly the most powerful weapon on the planet. He nodded to himself. It was probably that.

"Sorry, there are some things you shouldn't ask a girl, and that's one of them."

"You just made that up. Okay, Sandy. So, what's the deal with you and David? That last time I checked, you thought he was nice but a bit too geeky for the likes of you."

Sandy quickened her pace. It took Jefferson a few seconds to catch her up. "Or were my eyes playing tricks on me?"

"Jefferson," she whispered. "I don't want to die alone. Don't you get that?"

"What are you talking about, you're not going to die."

She nodded. "Yes, I am. It's raging through my body. There's nothing anyone can do to stop it. No human doctors, that's for sure."

"You don't know that. Anyway, you have us, and *what about your boyfriend*? The poor lad will be worried sick about you."

She took a deep breath. "There never was a boyfriend. I made him up to stop all the creeps that I work with from asking me out."

That statement just showed how much Jefferson knew about his friend. Christ, to think he was actually looking forward to their wedding. One thing was sure, the woman would make a terrific author. Just how much of her past conversations were real?

"How are you holding up?" Janine took his hand. "We're nearly there, honey."

"Will you be okay going back into the furniture shop? I know how bad it was for you in there."

"I haven't given it any thought. All that matters is that we'll be out of here and we're together. I'm glad to see Sandy helped you."

"Yeah, she sure has a way with words," he replied. "Sandy has always been good at getting people motivated. The company had sent her on half a dozen courses over the past few months. She was desperate to get out of that nail bar. God, listen to me banging on about such mundane bullshit. How weird is that, after everything that's happened to us."

She gently squeezed his hand. "It isn't weird at all, honey. It's perfectly normal behaviour. After this unbelievable clusterfuck, talking about the mundane will help your mind to adjust to our new circumstances." Janine stopped. She wrapped her arms around his waist. "Believe me. I'm not too sure I want to see what's happened outside the mall."

Her words helped his old anxieties resurface. She was right. After all, apart from him, nobody else had gotten in here. Add in the factor of all the power failing, it painted a very grim scenario. "We'll soon find out, Janine. We're almost at your shop."

Jefferson and Janine joined David and Sandy directly outside the store. Like the rest of the mall they had passed through, the store looked deserted. He stayed where he was and frowned at the sight before him. Somebody had been in here after he and Janine had fled. The bed which he'd taken refuge under now blocked the exit. Chairs, drawers, and even a large wardrobe were piled on top of the mattress.

"That is unexpected," said David.

Jefferson and Sandy ventured inside, followed by Janine and David. Somebody had tried to make damn sure that nobody was going to run out of here. It would take them ages to shift all that stuff. Jefferson stopped beside a display stand advertising cheap sofas. He could hear something. It sounded like a high-pitched hum. The noise was coming from that wardrobe. Jefferson turned to Sandy. "Can you hear that?"

The girl's gaze hadn't shifted from the blocked entrance. They now practically bulged in their sockets. "You have got to be shitting me!" she exclaimed.

He spun around to find they were no longer alone. That creepy janitor was now sitting on the wardrobe with his legs dangling over the edge. "What the hell is going on?"

"Apparently, it's called a field displacement procedure." Desmond chuckled. "Bet you all just shit your pants didn't you!"

He turned his attention to Sandy. "Hi there, honeypot. I can't tell you how happy I am to see you're still kicking about."

"Get out of our way, you freaky weirdo," she spat. "Haven't you got some bogs to clean or something?"

Desmond looked straight at Jefferson. "God, I love it when she talks mucky. It so turns me on."

Jefferson didn't like this one bit. His guts were rolling over again. This time with good reason. That janitor did not pull the magic trick without some help. He slowly took a single step back, silently wishing Sandy would do the same. "What do you want, Desmond?"

"Oh, that's easy." He reached into his back pocket and pulled out a small glass vial containing a bright blue liquid. Desmond gave it a little shake. "Your feisty friend isn't going to last much longer. Pretty soon all those pretty bits of hers will soon either drop off or turn into stinking mush, and there is absolutely nothing any of you can do about it." He gave the vial one more shake. "I can save your life, honeypot. All you have to do is be my princess. I'll even let all the others leave the mall. Now, you can't say fairer than that."

Sandy turned around. She looked straight at David, and then after a moment, she looked at the rest of them. "Guys, I'm really sorry about this, I truly am. Please forgive me?" The girl then spun around, aimed her gun at Desmond's grinning face, and fired. A stream of energy smashed into an invisible sphere encircling the man, who was now incandescent with rage. The wardrobe liquefied, throwing the janitor off the piled-up furniture. The man crashed onto the floor.

"You ungrateful little shit!" he screamed. "You're all going to get it. I'm so going to fix all your wagons now!" He jumped to his feet and glared at Sandy. "Watch this then, you smirking bitch. I'll show you some fucking field displacement thingy that you'll never forget." He made a point of dropping the glass vial before he pulled out a small black cube. "See you all in hell," he snarled, jabbing one of the cube sides.

That humming noise filled the room. One by one, the forms of several very large dinosaurs popped into existence directly in front of them.

"Run!" shouted Jefferson. He pulled back Sandy, threw her towards David, and then raced out of the furniture store with the sounds of two roaring Tyrannosaurs drowning out the noise of Desmond's manic laughter. He shot past Kevin who hadn't moved an inch. "Head for the main doors!" he yelled at the others. Jefferson turned around, fully aware that three of the predators were now heading straight for them. "Come on, man, for God's sake. You can't stop these things."

The large man took his eyes off the approaching Tyrannosaur for a second to push Jefferson away. "Go on, get away. Don't waste my fight!"

He saw a smaller creature, a raptor running past him and Kevin, keeping close to the shop fronts. It was going to jump straight onto Janine's head! "Thank you for this, man!" he shouted. Jefferson screamed at Janine to get out of the way while he pumped his legs, desperately trying to reach them before that raptor caught his Janine. He heard a scream of rage which quickly turned into a shriek of agony just as the raptor jumped onto the first eatery table. It used them like stepping stones, each pace taking it closer and closer to the woman he loved. Jefferson screamed again, but the roars of the huge killers behind him made it impossible for them to hear his warning.

One more leap and the raptor would be in amongst his friends. Jefferson bent down and scooped up a chewed-up bone lying in the middle of the concourse. With all his might, he threw it at the smaller dinosaur, shouting out in triumph when his missile smacked it right on the muzzle. The impact threw it off balance, and it skidded off the table and landed directly in the path of one of the tyrannosaurs. It lowered its head, grabbed the squawking creature, and bit it into three pieces without even slowing its pace.

"What are you going to do?" cried David. "The shutters are still down."

Jefferson shook his head and ran straight for the metal barriers. "Trust me," he shouted. "They never were down." He closed his eyes, hoping to God he was right about this, and quickened his pace while screaming hoarsely.

Bright sunlight stung his closed eyes. He opened one of them and screamed in terror at the sight of another Tyrannosaur running towards him from the other side of the deserted square. The dinosaur's foot slammed down onto the head of an old man; it didn't seem all that bothered about the abundance of human bodies lying everywhere.

"Get over here, you stupid kid!" yelled a voice coming from behind a parked-up military truck. "Come on, move your arse!"

Jefferson knew just how close that thing was to him, yet he couldn't go, not without the others. He spun around and managed to catch Janine in his open arms just as the noise of automatic gunfire reached his already battered ears. Her bulging eyes told Jefferson that that weren't out of danger just yet. He pulled her away from the pretend shutters just as Margaret ran out into the square and straight into the path of the wounded dinosaur.

"Get over here!" Jefferson shouted.

The woman either didn't hear him over the sounds of the rounds still tearing into the creature's thick hide or the very sight of the dinosaur froze her solid. The animal lowered its head and bit Margaret in two, cutting off her voice in mid-scream.

The remaining two survivors burst through, and they both slipped and fell into the lake of thick blood, gushing across the paving. It was only David's lightning reactions that saved them from being the Tyrannosaur's next victims.

Jefferson's friend wrapped his arm around Sandy's body and flipped her across his front before rolling away from what remained of the older woman's corpse. Both Jefferson ignored the shouts from the unknown newcomers and ran over to their friends and pulled them to safety just as the mortally wounded dinosaur finally died.

The officer, who Jefferson had seen earlier, leading the parade stormed over to the group, his face red with fury.

"You almost got yourself killed, you idiots. What on earth were you doing hiding beside those shutters? The warnings went off hours ago. This place is supposed to be clear of civilians now."

Jefferson just shook his head. He didn't have time for any of this bullshit. He tried to move away, only for another soldier to pull him back.

"The captain asked you a question, young lad. You'd better answer him."

"Get the fuck off me, you dickhead! We've just come out of the mall and there are…"

The soldier then slapped his face. "You'd just better watch your mouth."

Jefferson shook his head. "Fuck you." He spat warm blood into the soldier's face, just as he saw the familiar huge heads of their saurian pursuers pushing through the shutter illusion. The resulting shouts of the other soldiers made the one holding Jefferson turn around.

The soldier tried to raise his rifle but it was too late. Three raptors leapt at the man, their sickle-shaped hind claws shredding his body into ribbons of bleeding flesh. Jefferson grabbed the arm of the astonished captain and pulled him away from the raging dinosaurs.

One of the Tyrannosaurs had taken exception to the raptor stealing food out from under its snout and had tried to bite the little dinosaur which resulted in the other raptors jumping onto both larger dinosaurs.

Jefferson slammed his back against the other side of the truck while watching the rest of the squad take up position by the front of the vehicle. They all opened fire at the fighting animals. The bullets tore into their hides. The smaller animals were torn apart under the hail of weapons fire. One of the Tyrannosaurs had obviously had enough and retreated, limping away from the massacre. The remaining animal wasn't quite so easily scared.

It spun around and charged the truck. Sandy ran up and took position behind the soldiers who were still pumping round after round into the charging dinosaur with seemingly little effect. She then fired her strange weapon and the Tyrannosaur's mid-section just melted.

"I remember you winking at me," said Jefferson. "You probably don't remember that." The officer wasn't even looking at him anymore. His eyes were on Sandy, specifically on the alien gun. "We really were inside the shopping centre, you know."

The captain nodded, still not taking his eyes off Sandy. "Yeah, so I gathered. I'm supposed to take all civilians to the resource centre they've set up in the city library." He turned and looked into Jefferson's eyes. "I don't believe that any of you fall into that category anymore. Are you willing to help us contain this clusterfuck?"

Janine walked over to the captain. She stood beside Jefferson and took his hand. "Captain. You have absolutely no idea how bad this situation really is. If you can give us a few hours to get cleaned up, have something to eat and to grieve over the people we have lost, I promise we'll tell you everything we know."

## CHAPTER NINETEEN

From his vantage point on the roof of the shopping centre, Desmond watched the survivors and those soldiers fight off the dinosaurs. He waved at them and felt most annoyed when none of the buggers turned to wave back. With a bit of luck, a stray dinosaur might pick up their scent, sneak up on them and eat the ungrateful little shits. That'd show them.

Desmond saw a few other people in the city centre. Some were hiding as the expelled dinosaurs lumbered past them. There were certainly more dinosaurs than humans down there now. He walked close to the edge, trying to see if any of the females were pretty.

"What happened to the other one?" He looked at Zinik-Tow, who stood a few metres away, stroking Susan's head. It appeared that neither of them were too keen on heights.

"He and the rest of our species returned to the quantum capsule and displaced to another location on this planet. That is something I did not anticipate. He also took a lone female as well. I can only assume that he took her to experiment upon, to find a contagion more effective that the one he had already used on the native population."

"Wait, are you telling me that we all might still die?"

"That is the logical scenario."

Desmond sat on the edge of the roof, watching his lost love take the hand of the geek and walk away from the shopping centre. "Why isn't Sandy dead?"

"I do not know. It is possible that she will not die of the contagion. If that is the case, then the contagion has altered her at a genetic level. It means that if that woman breeds, the offspring are likely to be mutants, even giving rise to another species."

Desmond turned from the roof and walked over to Zinik-Tow and Susan. He grinned to himself. "Well, isn't that the ultimate irony!"

# EPILOGUE

Gloria Chadburn sipped her iced tea while watching Jane's little darlings tear into the nest of rats they'd found in the barn behind the big house. They'd brought their bodies back and dropped them into a pile in front of their mother first. Of course, Jane took the largest corpse for herself before allowing her offspring to feed on the remaining bodies. Gloria found it rather sweet to watch such motherly love. Of course, she wasn't that happy watching Jane's knitted blue sweater getting covered in dirty rat blood. She sighed to herself. It wasn't that much of a disaster, though. Gloria could always knit the raptor another sweater.

The boys were talking about the war as per usual; it's all they ever seemed to talk about nowadays. Honestly, after two years of fighting, she thought the three factions would have made up and become friends by now. It all seemed rather silly.

Dailess-Zaid, his creepy little second-in-command, Quediss-Tel, plus one of the soldiers from the warrior caste were sat around the other garden table. Dailess-Zaid was not happy that somehow Sons of Maulis-Bow had managed to contaminate their clone vats. Consequently, the next batch of ten thousand warriors had to be terminated. He was under the impression that the human faction had rendered the terrorists practically extinct with the last salvo of nuclear missiles they had used against them.

Gloria leaned down and pulled one of Jane's babies back when he got a little too close to the soldier. She caught the eye of Dailess-Zaid and smiled at him, feeling a little flutter in her stomach when the Saurion gave her a nod in return. He told her last night that he had a surprise announcement to make today, involving her. She couldn't wait to find out what it was.

# THE END?

 SEVEREDPRESS

facebook.com/severedpress
twitter.com/severedpress

## CHECK OUT OTHER GREAT DINOSAUR THRILLERS

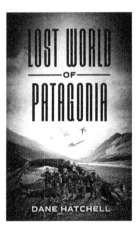

## LOST WORLD OF PATAGONIA
## by Dane Hatchell

An earthquake opens a path to a land hidden for millions of years. Under the guise of finding cryptid animals, Ace Corporation sends Alex Klasse, a Cryptozoologist and university professor, his associates, and a band of mercenaries to explore the Lost World of Patagonia. The crew boards a nuclear powered All-Terrain Tracked Carrier and takes a harrowing ride into the unknown.

The expedition soon discovers prehistoric creatures still exist. But the dangers won't prevent a sub-team from leaving the group in search of rare jewels. Tensions run high as personalities clash, and man proves to be just as deadly as the dinosaurs that roam the countryside.

Lost World of Patagonia is a prehistoric thriller filled with murder, mayhem, and savage dinosaur action.

## SAVAGE ISLAND
## by Alan Spencer

Somewhere in the Atlantic Ocean, an uncharted island has been used for the illegal dumping of chemicals and pollutants for years by Globo Corp's. Private investigator Pierce Range will learn plenty about the evil conglomerate when Susan Branch, an environmentalist from The Green Project, hires him to join the expedition to save her kidnapped father from Globo Corp's evil hands.

Things go to hell in a hurry once the team reaches the island. The bloodthirsty dinosaurs and voracious cannibals are only the beginning of the fight for survival. Pierce must unlock the mysteries surrounding the toxic operation and somehow remain in one piece to complete the rescue mission.

Ratchet up the body count, because this mission will leave the killing floor soaked in blood and chewed up corpses. When the insane battle ends, will there by anybody left alive to survive Savage Island?

SEVEREDPRESS

facebook.com/severedpress
twitter.com/severedpress

# CHECK OUT OTHER GREAT DINOSAUR THRILLERS

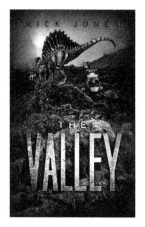

## THE VALLEY
### by Rick Jones

In a dystopian future, a self-contained valley in Argentina serves as the 'far arena' for those convicted of a crime. Inside the Valley: carnivorous dinosaurs generated from preserved DNA. The goal: cross the Valley to get to the Gates of Freedom. The chance of survival: no one has ever completed the journey. Convicted of crimes with little or no merit, Ben Peyton and others must battle their way across fields filled with the world's deadliest apex predators in order to reach salvation. All the while the journey is caught on cameras and broadcast to the world as a reality show, the deaths and killings real, the macabre appetite of the audience needing to be satiated as Ben Peyton leads his team to escape not only from a legal system that's more interested in entertainment than in justice, but also from the predators of the Valley.

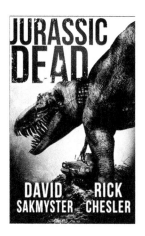

## JURASSIC DEAD
### by Rick Chesler & David Sakmyster

An Antarctic research team hoping to study microbial organisms in an underground lake discovers something far more amazing: perfectly preserved dinosaur corpses. After one thaws and wakes ravenously hungry, it becomes apparent that death, like life, will find a way.
Environmental activist Alex Ramirez, son of the expedition's paleontologist, came to Antarctica to defend the organisms from extinction, but soon learns that it is the human race that needs protecting.

# SEVEREDPRESS

 facebook.com/severedpress
 twitter.com/severedpress

## CHECK OUT OTHER GREAT DINOSAUR THRILLERS

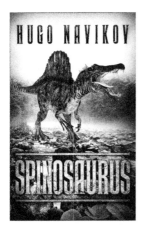

### SPINOSAURUS
### by Hugo Navikov

Brett Russell is a hunter of the rarest game. His targets are cryptids, animals denied by science. But they are well known by those living on the edges of civilization, where monsters attack and devour their animals and children and lay ruin to their shantytowns.
When a shadowy organization sends Brett to the Congo in search of the legendary dinosaur cryptid Kasai Rex, he will face much more than a terrifying monster from the past. Spinosaurus is a dinosaur thriller packed with intrigue, action and giant prehistoric predators.

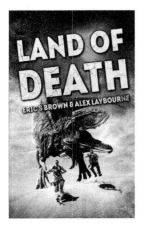

### LAND OF DEATH
### by Eric S Brown & Alex Laybourne

A group of American soldiers, fleeing an organized attack on their base camp in the Middle East, encounter a storm unlike anything they've seen before. When the storm subsides, they wake up to find themselves no longer in the desert and perhaps not even on Earth. The jungle they've been deposited in is a place ruled by prehistoric creatures long extinct. Each day is a struggle to survive as their ammo begins to run low and virtually everything they encounter, in this land they've been hurled into, is a deadly threat.

# SEVEREDPRESS

facebook.com/severedpress
twitter.com/severedpress

## CHECK OUT OTHER GREAT DINOSAUR THRILLERS

### WRITTEN IN STONE
### by David Rhodes

Charles Dawson is trapped 100 million years in the past. Trying to survive from day to day in a world of dinosaurs he devises a plan to change his fate. As he begins to write messages in the soft mud of a nearby stream, he can only hope they will be found by someone who can stop his time travel. Professor Ron Fontana and Professor Ray Taggit, scientists with opposing views, each discover the fossilized messages. While attempting to save Charles, Professor Fontana, his daughter Lauren and their friend Danny are forced to join Taggit and his group of mercenaries. Taggit does not intend to rescue Charles Dawson, but to force Dawson to travel back in time to gather samples for Taggit's fame and fortune. As the two groups jump through time they find they must work together to make it back alive as this fast-paced thriller climaxes at the very moment the age of dinosaurs is ending.

### HARD TIME
### by Alex Laybourne

Rookie officer Peter Malone and his heavily armed team are sent on a deadly mission to extract a dangerous criminal from a classified prison world. A Kruger Correctional facility where only the hardest, most vicious criminals are sent to fend for themselves, never to return.

But when the team come face to face with ancient beasts from a lost world, their mission is changed. The new objective: Survive.

 SEVERED**PRESS**

facebook.com/severedpress
twitter.com/severedpress

## CHECK OUT OTHER GREAT DINOSAUR THRILLERS

### JURASSIC ISLAND
by Viktor Zarkov

Guided by satellite photos and modern technology a ragtag group of survivalists and scientists travel to an uncharted island in the remote South Indian Ocean. Things go to hell in a hurry once the team reaches the island and the massive megalodon that attacked their boats is only the beginning of their desperate fight for survival.

Nothing could have prepared billionaire explorer Joseph Thornton and washed up archaeologist Christopher "Colt" McKinnon for the terrifying prehistoric creatures that wait for them on JURASSIC ISLAND!

### K-REX
by L.Z. Hunter

Deep within the Congo jungle, Circuitz Mining employs mercenaries as security for its Coltan mining site. Armed with assault rifles and decades of experience, nothing should go wrong. However, the dangers within the jungle stretch beyond venomous snakes and poisonous spiders. There is more to fear than guerrillas and vicious animals. Undetected, something lurks under the expansive treetop canopy...

Something ancient.

Something dangerous.

Kasai Rex!

Printed in Great Britain
by Amazon